MY HEART

FELL IN BATTLEFIELD

SOLDIER'S LOVE FOR SUSPECTED KASHMIRI SPY

MURARI KUMAR

Clever Fox® PUBLISHING
Chennai • Bangalore

CLEVER FOX PUBLISHING
Chennai, India

Published by CLEVER FOX PUBLISHING 2025

ISBN: 978-93-6707-462-6

Declaration

"This is a work of fiction, inspired by the events of terrorism in Jammu & Kashmir and ceasefire violations on India-Pakistan Line of Control, but not intended as a factual account. Names, characters, places, events, locales, and incidents are either the products of the author's imagination or used in a fictitious manner. Any resemblance to actual persons, living or dead, or actual events is purely coincidental. While the author has strived for accuracy in military details, some aspects may be fictionalized for narrative purposes. This book is intended for entertainment purposes and does not represent any real-world military personnel or units in a negative light and any perceived similarities are unintentional. The author aims to explore the human experience of battle and the impact of conflict on individuals and societies."

Contents

Prologue

“Pink Tiffin Box Under Mortar Shelling.”

September 16, 2014–1640 hrs

The first shell landed thirty meters short of our bunker at 1640 hours.

I was holding a volleyball, about to serve for match point, when the ground beneath my boots suddenly wasn’t there anymore. My body hit the dirt before my brain processed the whistling sound that meant death was falling from the sky. The volleyball bounced once and rolled away—such a stupid thing to notice when 120mm mortar bombs were raining down on us.

“Take cover!” I shouted, but my men were already scrambling. Lance Naik Dhawan dove behind the cook house. Sepoy Rajesh disappeared into the nearest bunker like he’d been swallowed whole. These weren’t fresh recruits—they’d heard that sound before and felt the earth shake when Pakistani gunners decided to remind us they were watching.

The second and third shells hit in rapid succession. Classic mortar pattern—three rounds from each tube, coordinated fire from a Pakistani mortar platoon. Much closer.

The post-monsoon air was crisp and clear, offering perfect visibility across the valley—which meant perfect targeting conditions for both sides. The explosion sucked all the air from my lungs, replaced it with dust and the metallic taste of fear. My ears rang like temple bells, but underneath that noise, I could hear something worse—the wet sound of dirt and rocks raining down on our tin roof. A piece of shrapnel, hot enough to brand cattle, landed two inches from my left boot.

My body moved before my mind caught up. Distance: 470 meters from their nearest position. Trajectory: high angle, probably from the ridge behind Hill 4590. Pattern: three rounds per mortar, coordinated platoon fire. That meant they had at least three Type 86 120mm mortars working us over—Chinese-made tubes that had become standard in Pakistani light artillery. They were ranging us, walking their fire closer with each salvo to find the sweet spot where our bunker used to be.

I pressed my face against the cold mud, tasting earth and my own sweat. The smell of cordite mixed with the pine scent from the surrounding forest. Another shell screamed overhead—closer still. The impact made my teeth rattle in my skull and sent vibrations through my chest like someone was playing drums on my ribcage.

"Sir!" Havildar Sanjay's voice cut through the chaos. "Communication line's down!"

Of course, it was. The bastards knew exactly what they were doing—cut our communications first, then work us over until we were too dead to call for help. I crawled toward the fire control bunker, my knees scraping against sharp stones, uniform soaking up mud like a sponge.

The shelling continued until 0130 hours. Six hours of hell—salvos of three mortar bombs every few minutes, the Pakistani mortar platoon methodically working over our position. We lost two tents, half our equipment, and what was left of my nerves. But we were alive, which in this business counted as a victory.

The moment the last mortar bomb exploded, I was moving. As the artillery Observation Post officer, I had work to do. No time to catch my breath or check for wounds—the enemy had just given away their position, and now it was our turn to bite back.

"Havildar Sanjay, with me!" I called, grabbing my binoculars and range finder. My legs felt unsteady after six hours of hugging the ground, but instinct took over. I scrambled up the rocky slope to our observation post—a reinforced position with clear sightlines to the Pakistani ridges.

My hands moved automatically, setting up the artillery board and plotting coordinates. Through my binoculars, I could see the telltale dust clouds still hanging over Hill 4590 where their mortars had fired from. Grid reference: Papa Kilo 157439. Range: 4,200 meters. Perfect target for our 120 mm mortars back at the base.

I cranked the magneto phone, the familiar whirring sound somehow comforting after the chaos. "Fire Control, this is Mendhar OP. Fire mission. Grid Papa Kilo 157439. Enemy mortar position. Three tubes were observed firing. Request immediate suppression."

"Mendhar OP, Fire Control. Shot, over."

"Shot, out." I pressed the binoculars to my eyes, watching the ridge through the green-tinted lenses.

Thirty-seven seconds later, I heard the distinctive crump of our own mortars firing from base camp, followed by the whistle of bombs arcing overhead. I held my breath, counting—

The first salvo landed fifty meters short of the enemy position. Close, but not close enough.

"Fire Control, Mendhar OP. Add 50, fire for effect."

"Add 50, fire for effect, out."

Our second salvo was beautiful—three HE bombs landing right in their firing position. I watched through my binoculars as dirt and debris erupted from the ridge, hopefully sending the Pakistani mortar crews scrambling for cover or better yet, to meet their maker.

"Fire Control, Mendhar OP. Target destroyed. End of mission. Good shooting."

For the first time in six hours, I allowed myself a grim smile. The bastards had woken up the wrong artillery officer tonight.

By 0220, I'd crawled back down to our magneto phone at the command post—that reliable old German invention from the 1870s that still worked when modern radios failed. Hand-cranked electricity, no batteries needed, perfect for maintaining radio silence when the enemy was listening. The brass casing felt cold and solid in my hands as I cranked the handle and waited for the connection.

"Thunder Base, this is Mendhar Forward. We're operational but need immediate resupply. Ammunition, medical supplies, and rations. Over."

"Mendhar Forward, Thunder Base. Resupply approved. ETA 0400 hours via mule train. Maintain position. Over."

The mules arrived just as the first pale light began creeping over the mountains. Poor animals looked as tired as we felt, picking their way carefully down the rocky path with panniers full of life-saving supplies. The handlers moved like ghosts in the pre-dawn darkness, speaking in whispers and hand signals.

I was inventorying ammunition boxes when Naik Pathaniya appeared at my elbow. Good soldier, steady under fire, but right now he looked confused about something.

"Saab," he said, holding out a bright pink container that looked like it had been teleported from another planet. "Madam ne bheja hai."

I stared at the thing. In a world of olive drab and camouflage, this pink tiffin box was like a flower blooming in a minefield. My first thought was IED—improvised explosive device. Some clever Pakistani intelligence officer had figured out how to weaponize lunch.

"Kis madam ne?" I asked, my voice sharper than I intended.

"Saab, pata nahi," Pathaniya shrugged. "Base camp mein diya tha."

"Step back," I ordered, carrying the tiffin box away from the bunker. My pulse hammered against my ribs—not from fear, but from the strange mix of curiosity and suspicion that was making my heart beat faster than the mortar fire had.

I set it down on open ground and called for the metal detector. The device beeped steadily as Havildar Sanjay swept it over the container—no change in pitch, no warning signals. Just the normal sounds of a lunch box being a lunch box.

"Get Darpan," I called to the K-9, sniffer dog handler.

Our sniffer dog came trotting over, tail wagging like this was all a game. But instead of alerting to explosives, Darpan started drooling and licking the outside of the container. His entire body wiggled with excitement, the way he only did when someone was cooking chicken or gosht.

"Well, that settles it," I muttered, cleaning the container with water from my cookhouse. The steam rose like incense as I carefully opened the lid.

Nihari gosht. Real, honest-to-God home-cooked mutton nihari. The smell hit me like a physical force—turmeric and coriander, garam masala and fresh cilantro. My mouth turned to desert sand with sudden hunger.

But who would send this? I ran through the possibilities like targeting coordinates. Five kilometers: nobody. Ten kilometers: still nobody. Fifteen, thirty, fifty kilometers: no women in my life who even knew where I was posted.

Wait. Fifty-six kilometers. Mandi, in Poonch district.

Dr. Jasleen Kaur.

The name hit me like a ricochet. I could see her face in my mind—those dark eyes that seemed to hold secrets, the way she'd looked at me during the Poonch Linkup Day ceremony before everything went sideways. Before the intelligence officers pulled us apart like we were dangerous chemicals that might explode if mixed.

But why would she send food to a forward combat position? Why risk her already shaky status with the authorities? The woman was suspected of being a Pakistani spy, for God's sake. Sending gosht to an Indian Army officer wasn't exactly the behavior of someone trying to keep a low profile.

My field phone buzzed—two short bursts. The resupply team at base camp.

"Saab," came the voice of Havildar Ramesh, "Tiffin box bheja hai aapke liye. Kal ek civilian madam lekar aayi thi.

Hamne unka pura detail le liya aur khana bhi nursing assistant ne check kar liya tha."

So she'd come personally. Walked up to our administrative base, past three checkpoints and at least a dozen suspicious soldiers, just to deliver lunch to a man she barely knew. A man who'd stood by and watched while she was arrested.

I ate the gosht slowly, but it had gone cold during the long journey. The taste was strange on my tongue—still delicious, but somehow different when eaten in a bunker that reeked of cordite and fear. My mind calculated the logistics: how had she managed this delivery? My heart warmed at the simple kindness, while battlefield intuition screamed warnings about security breaches and inappropriate contact. Three parts of me—tongue, mind, and heart—all pulling in different directions, like a three-way tug of war I couldn't win.

After finishing, I lay back on my cot, staring at the corrugated metal ceiling of my bunker. The pink tiffin box sat on my field desk like an accusation. Outside, I could hear my men cleaning weapons and checking defenses. Normal sounds of military life, but somehow they felt different now.

My body was exhausted from the shelling, but my mind wouldn't shut down. Blood rushed in my ears like distant artillery, making it impossible to think clearly. Why would Dr. Jasleen Kaur risk everything to send me home-cooked food? What was she trying to tell me? And why did the thought of her kindness terrify me more than Pakistani mortars ever could? I closed my eyes and tried to sleep, but all I could see was her face. Those eyes that might belong to a spy, or might belong to someone who simply cared whether I lived or died in this godforsaken valley.

The empty pink container seemed to glow in the darkness, a bright spot of color in a world painted in shades of camouflage and compromise. Tomorrow I'd have to decide what it meant. Tonight, I just held onto the warmth of being cared for by someone who had no reason to care at all.

**Steel birds screamed from distant heights,*
Earth shook beneath my trembling feet.
Then came soft gift through smoke and fright—
Pink box that made my dread complete.

Her kindness pierced the battle's roar,
A gentle hand through cannon's thunder.
This stranger's care worth fighting for,
*Her ghost now haunts each night I wonder.**

CHAPTER 1

"OFFICER AND GENTLEMAN IN POONCH"

Eighteen months earlier - June 15, 2013

The military convoy rumbled to a stop at Poonch cantonment, dust settling around the olive-green vehicles. I stepped out of the truck, my new artillery officer's uniform still crisp despite the journey from Jammu. The summer heat hit me immediately—35°C of dry mountain air that carried the scent of pine and dust from the winding roads. The weight of my kit bag felt substantial, but nothing compared to the sense of responsibility now settling on my shoulders.

A jeep pulled up, more dust swirling around its tires. The driver jumped out and saluted smartly. "Lieutenant Murari, sir? I'm Naik Pathaniya. Welcome to Poonch."

The moment I stepped onto Poonch soil, the mountain breeze cut through my uniform, carrying with it the weight of history and expectation. My name is Lieutenant Murari Kumar, fresh out of the Indian Military Academy, and my pulse hammered with a mixture of excitement and terror. I hadn't felt since my first parade at IMA.

Those mountains around me—massive, snow-capped giants watching over everything—they'd seen countless wars and acts of bravery before I ever showed up. Just looking at them made my chest tighten with a feeling I couldn't name.

June 2013. That date is burned into my brain just like the regimental insignia I wore with such pride. My first posting with the Artillery Regiment had begun, and let me tell you—the jump from being a cadet dreaming of glory to an officer with actual lives depending on me? That hit harder than any drill sergeant ever could.

My unit was located inside the Baldev Mahal Complex, a significant architectural ensemble built by Raja Baldev Singh, reflecting the grandeur of Dogra heritage in Poonch. It included multiple structures, some of which were severely damaged during the 2005 earthquake and have since fallen into aging deterioration.

The barracks were nothing special—plain, functional, a total contrast to the gorgeous green valleys all around us.

The Commanding Officer's order was clear: "Live with your men, Lieutenant. Eat their food and share their hardships. Respect is earned, not inherited with rank. Every morning when that whistle ripped me from sleep, I was up alongside them at 0500 hrs. I figured they'd respect me more for the hardship we shared than for the lieutenant stars on my shoulders.

My God, those instructors were relentless. The Gunnery Instructor especially—a weathered JCO (Junior Commissioned Officer) with eyes that had seen too much death—he hammered artillery science into my brain until I could calculate firing trajectories half-asleep. Those massive Howitzer, became like extensions of my own body. I absorbed everything—every mechanism, every procedure, every possible failure—because I knew someday, someone's life would depend on me getting it right.

The 2IC and Adjutant watched me like hawks. When they occasionally nodded approval, it felt better than winning gold. Three months of training didn't just change what I knew—it changed who I was. That soft-spoken boy from Sainik School Goalpara hardened into something else entirely—an artillery officer ready to face whatever this border threw at me.

My Commanding Officer sent me to Brigade Headquarters to understand how things worked in the area. It is located in the **Moti Mahal** in Poonch, a stunning historical palace built between 1926 and 1936 during the reign of the Dogra Rajas. It was designed in a Scottish architectural style, featuring ivy-covered walls and intricate Kashmiri woodwork. The palace was initiated by Raja Sukhdev Singh and later completed by Raja Jagat Dev Singh, with British engineers overseeing its construction. It remains an important landmark in Poonch, reflecting the region's rich history and royal legacy.

As I read through history, current situations and intelligence reports describing the challenges—constant vigilance against infiltrators, the ever-present threat of terrorism, and the problem of anti-national elements—I felt my perspective shift. The beautiful landscape outside the window wasn't just scenery anymore; it was a battlefield where enemies could be hiding in plain sight.

"Trust is a luxury here, Lieutenant Murari," **Major Isaac**, the intelligence officer of the Poonch brigade, told me with an intense stare. "Verify everything, question everyone. Even the most innocent interactions can have implications for national security."

The summer wind howled through the valley, carrying the whispers of a thousand untold stories. Standing on that desolate road with the weight of my first real command pressing down on me, I finally understood what my instructors at the Academy meant when they talked about the "burden of the stars" on our shoulders.

This was Poonch—beautiful and brutal, peaceful and scarred. And I had only just begun to understand the complex web of duty, danger, and dedication that would define my days in this frontier outpost, where every sunrise brought both hope and uncertainty in equal measure.

**These ancient peaks where eagles soar*
Welcomed my Lieutenant's dream.
Baldev Mahal's weathered door
Opened to duty's pristine scheme.

From Goalpara's gentle fields
To Kashmir's stark and guarded line,
My uniform now bears the shield
*Of borders that are yours and mine.**

CHAPTER 2

"THUNDER AND PRECISION"

Aug–October 2013

Dawn broke over our artillery position like someone had spilled gold across the jagged horizon. I stood among the massive howitzers, their long barrels pointing skyward like accusing fingers. The gun area buzzed with focused energy as soldiers moved with practiced precision, each man a vital part of this well-oiled machine of destructive power.

"Battery Fire!" The call rang out, and instantly, the atmosphere changed. Calculated chaos erupted as coordinates were confirmed, charges prepared, and the massive breech swung open to accept the shell. I felt that familiar surge of adrenaline as the countdown began. Even in practice, the thunderous voice of an artillery piece speaking its deadly language shook not just the ground but something primal inside me.

"Fire!"

The concussion hit my chest before the sound reached my ears—a physical force that seemed to compress time itself. The shell arced away toward a distant practice target, leaving behind that acrid smell of cordite that clung to my uniform like a second skin. This was power. This was responsibility. This was the dance of death and defense that defined the path I'd chosen.

As August melted into September, the oppressive heat began to give way to something more bearable. The mornings carried a hint of coolness that whispered of the approaching autumn, though the afternoons still blazed with summer fury.

During a rare moment of free time, I found myself drawn to the ancient Buda Amarnath Temple. The structure had weathered centuries yet stood defiant against time and conflict, seeming to embody the resilience of this contested land. Inside, the cool darkness and lingering scent of incense offered a sanctuary from the constant vigilance required outside its walls.

An elderly priest watched me with knowing eyes as I stood before the shrine, my uniform out of place among the colorful devotees.

"Young officer," he said, his Hindi melodious with the regional accent, "you guard our borders, but here, even you are protected." His gnarled hand gestured toward the sacred flame. "Some battles are fought with weapons, others with faith. Both require courage."

His words stuck with me as I left, the temple bells echoing across the valley like a reminder of timeless truths amid temporary conflicts.

My first visit to the Line of Control stripped away any romantic notions about borders I might have had. The LoC wasn't just a line on a map but a wound across the landscape—concrete bunkers, coils of razor wire, and watchtowers standing in stark contrast to the breathtaking beauty surrounding them. Through my binoculars, I could see Pakistani positions mirroring our own, each side watching, waiting, wondering.

"They're having chai right now, just like us," my commanding officer remarked, following my gaze. "Same mountains, same weather, same concerns about what their family is doing back home." He lowered his binoculars. "Never forget that, Lieutenant. The enemy is human.

Underestimate that humanity, and you underestimate the threat they pose."

Not far from this symbol of separation stood Nagali Sahib Gurudwara, where divisions seemed to dissolve in shared devotion. Sikh soldiers from our unit removed their boots and covered their heads alongside local worshippers, the langar serving meals without regard for rank or religion. In the golden light of the prayer hall, I saw another face of Kashmir—one where harmony wasn't just possible but practiced.

At Chakan Da Bagh Gate, that philosophy became real before my eyes. The gateway between nations stood as both bridge and barrier—a narrow passage where strictly controlled trade and occasional humanitarian exchanges happened amid layers of security and suspicion. Watching civilians from both sides exchange goods under the watchful eyes of armed personnel, I witnessed the strange dance of hostility and necessity that characterized life in a divided region.

October arrived with a painter's palette of colors—the chinar leaves turning brilliant gold and crimson, the air sharp enough to cut, and morning frost that warned of harder days ahead. The mountains seemed to move closer, their white peaks more defined against crystalline skies.

As the days grew shorter and the bite in the air grew sharper, anticipation began building throughout the unit. November would bring the annual Poonch Linkup Day celebration— a major event requiring months of preparation. The historical significance wasn't lost on any of us; this ceremony honored the brave defense of Poonch during the 1947–48 war when Brigadier Pritam Singh had held the line against overwhelming odds.

As the weeks passed, my uniform began to feel less like a costume and more like a second skin. The weight of my weapon became comforting rather than cumbersome. The face that looked back at me from my shaving mirror each morning showed subtle changes—lines of responsibility etching themselves around eyes that had grown more watchful, more aware.

By late October, preparation for the ceremony dominated our daily routine. The historic Moti Mahal buzzed with activity as advance teams checked sound systems, prepared guest accommodations, and coordinated with civil authorities. I found myself assigned to protocol duties—a mixed blessing that meant less field time but more interaction with the complex web of military and civilian dignitaries who would attend.

Then came the announcement that stirred something deep in my chest, the guest list for the November 21st ceremony. What had been just another page in my military history textbooks was about to become a lived experience. The celebration would commemorate the brave defense of Poonch during the 1947–48 war, and the Poonch ALG (Advance Landing Ground) would once again serve as a crucial venue for demonstrating our military capabilities and honoring our heritage.

The historic Moti Mahal, once a royal residence now repurposed as a symbol of Poonch's enduring significance, buzzed with activity as preparations intensified. Being the junior-most officer had its disadvantages—I was tasked with coordinating guest arrangements, checking sound systems, and ensuring the parade ground at ALG was immaculate.

"The guest list, Lieutenant," my superior handed me several pages of names. "Familiarize yourself. You'll be greeting some of them personally."

That evening, as the first real cold snap of the season settled over our camp, I sat in my quarters reviewing the ceremonial protocols. The guest list seemed endless—military dignitaries, civil administrators, local leaders, representatives from various community organizations. Each name represented someone whose comfort and security would be my responsibility.

I ran my finger down the columns of dignitaries, local leaders, and special invitees. Wind rattled my windows as I studied each entry, memorizing names and designations that would be crucial for the ceremony. Then my finger stopped, and something cold that had nothing to do with the weather ran down my spine.

"Dr. Jasleen Kaur"

The designation "Medical Officer, District Hospital" followed her name, along with a note indicating she would be recognized for exceptional medical service to both civilian and military personnel in the region.

Outside, the night carried the first hint of the winter that would soon grip these mountains. But inside my quarters, staring at that name on the guest list, I felt something entirely different beginning to stir—a warmth that had nothing to do with the kerosene heater in the corner and everything to do with anticipation I couldn't quite name.

Sleep just wouldn't come that night. As I lay under my blanket, listening to the distant calls of night patrols, my mind kept creating images of Dr. Kaur. Would she be stern and clinical, shaped by emergency surgeries and difficult decisions? Or perhaps compassionate and warm, having chosen to serve in this challenging region rather than pursue a lucrative practice in Delhi or Chandigarh?

Yet as consciousness finally began to fade, her name echoed in my thoughts like a half-remembered melody.

"Dr. Jasleen Kaur," I whispered into the darkness, the name somehow feeling significant on my tongue, as though speaking it aloud had set some invisible force into motion.

Morning would come too soon, bringing with it the final preparations for a ceremony that would change everything. But for now, in that space between wakefulness and dreams, I allowed myself to wonder about the woman behind the name—a name that, for reasons I couldn't yet understand, had already carved itself into my consciousness with the precision of an artillery coordinate, marking a target I hadn't known I was seeking.

**Howitzers teach their deadly song,*
Each shell a word I learn to speak.
At Budha Amarnath temple, prayers belong
To warriors both strong and weak.

Then came a name upon the page—
"Dr. Jasleen Kaur"—like dawn's first light.
Why does this stranger's script engage
*My soldier's heart before first sight?**

❀❀❀

CHAPTER 3

"WHEN EYES FIRST MET ACROSS THE PARADE"

November 21, 2013

The morning of Poonch Linkup Day arrived with an electric buzz in the air. Frost clung to the parade ground like scattered diamonds, and my breath formed small clouds as I checked the final arrangements. November mountain air bit through my dress uniform, sharp and clean.

Military vehicles gleamed in the early light, flags snapped in the crisp breeze, and soldiers stood in perfect formation awaiting the arrival of VIPs. The ceremony would honor those who had fought to protect Poonch during the 1947–48 war—heroes whose sacrifice had kept this strategic town from falling into enemy hands.

As the officer assigned to guest reception, I positioned myself near the entrance arch, guestlist card in hand, mentally reviewing notes about each important visitor. The Brigadier would arrive first, followed by senior civil administrators, then community leaders.

"They're starting to arrive, sir," Sepoy Rajesh informed me, pointing toward an approaching convoy.

I straightened my already perfect uniform and prepared to execute my duties with military precision. The Brigadier emerged from the lead vehicle, resplendent in his dress uniform adorned with medals that told stories of bravery and service.

"Everything in order, Lieutenant Murari?" he inquired as I saluted.

"Yes, sir. All arrangements as per protocol," I responded, handing him the first ceremonial bouquet.

The procession of dignitaries continued—district magistrate, police superintendent, local MLAs, each receiving appropriate military courtesies as they entered the venue. I checked names off my list methodically, my mind automatically cataloging faces, measuring security threats, calculating crowd flow patterns.

Then time seemed to slow.

A light pink kurta suit caught my eye among the arriving guests. Dr. Jasleen Kaur stepped out of a red Maruti car, and the reality of her presence far exceeded anything my imagination had conjured during those sleepless nights.

Her hair caught the morning light like spun silk, framing a face that seemed to blend classical Indian beauty with modern confidence. She moved with the natural grace of someone comfortable in her own skin, acknowledging greetings with a smile that transformed her entire face.

For a disorienting moment, I forgot my duties, my training, even where I stood. Something fundamental shifted within me—a recognition that went beyond physical attraction. It was as if I'd been searching for something without knowing what it was, and had suddenly found it walking across a parade ground in Poonch.

"Lieutenant? The bouquet?" The Brigadier's voice jolted me back to reality.

"Yes, sir." I said, hastily handing him the flower arrangement intended for Dr. Kaur.

My pulse hammered as I watched the Brigadier present the bouquet with formal courtesy. Dr. Kaur accepted with grace, her smile brightening as she thanked him in accented English that carried the musical quality of educated Kashmiri speech.

As protocol dictated, I led her to her designated position for the ceremony, conscious of maintaining professional behavior despite the unexpected turbulence in my chest.

"First time at Poonch Linkup Day, Doctor?" I asked, finding my voice surprisingly steady.

"No, Lieutenant," she replied, her voice melodious yet precise. "I've been in Poonch for years. The hospital keeps me quite busy, but I wouldn't miss this historical commemoration."

"This ceremony honors those who fought to protect civilians during the first Kashmir conflict," I explained, grateful for the neutral topic. "Many of the older residents still remember being relieved after months of siege."

"History that still lives in people's memories carries special power," she observed thoughtfully. "As a doctor, I see how past trauma shapes present health—both for individuals and communities."

Her insight revealed depth that complemented her beauty. This wasn't merely a young professional fulfilling a social obligation; this was someone who understood the complex tapestry of regional challenges. I found myself genuinely curious about her thoughts and her experiences.

The ceremony proceeded with military precision—speeches honoring fallen heroes, a parade showcasing current capabilities, and cultural performances celebrating the region's resilience. Throughout, I found my attention repeatedly drawn to Dr. Kaur, watching how she engaged fully with each element of the program.

During the pipe band performance, I noticed her tapping her foot subtly to the rhythm. When veterans shared their testimonies, her expression reflected genuine emotion—not the polite attention of someone enduring a duty, but real engagement with their stories.

When the formal ceremony concluded and guests moved toward the refreshment area, I found myself strategically positioned near her path.

"Did you enjoy the ceremony, Doctor?" I asked as she approached.

"Very much," she replied. "Particularly the veterans' testimonies. Medical school teaches anatomy and pharmacology, but understanding a community's collective memory helps me treat patients more effectively."

Before I could respond, my radio crackled with a request from the Brigadier for assistance with protocol arrangements. I excused myself reluctantly, duty once again taking precedence over personal inclination.

Throughout the remainder of the event, our paths crossed occasionally. Each brief exchange added another layer to my growing fascination. When she mentioned treating patients from both sides of local conflicts without asking about their political affiliations, I saw a glimpse of moral courage that impressed me more than any medal could.

During the cultural program on the lawn, she stood near a group of local women, and I overheard her speaking fluent Kashmiri with an elderly lady who was praising her for treating her grandson's injuries. The warmth in her voice and the respectful way she addressed the elder—painted a picture of someone deeply connected to this community.

As the event drew toward its close, I felt an unexpected sense of urgency. The day had passed too quickly, and opportunities for interaction had been too few. I watched as Dr. Kaur thanked the Brigadier and turned toward the exit, her departure seeming to dim the atmosphere.

In that moment, I realized how completely this woman—still virtually a stranger—had captured my attention. It wasn't merely her striking looks, though those were undeniable. It was the glimpses of character revealed through brief exchanges, the evident dedication to her profession, and the thoughtful engagement with the community she served.

As she disappeared from view, I stood there amid the dispersing crowd, aware that something significant had shifted in my world. The routine concerns of military life—equipment checks, duty rosters, patrol schedules—suddenly felt inadequate to contain what I was feeling.

"Saab, are you alright? You look like someone who just saw a ghost."

I turned to face his concerned expression. "Not a ghost, Pathaniya. Something much more dangerous."

He looked puzzled but didn't press the matter. Military men learn when not to ask questions.

That afternoon, as I completed my duty reports in the quiet of my quarters, I found myself replaying every moment of our interactions. Her laugh when a child had stumbled during the cultural program. The way she'd instinctively steadied an elderly veteran who had swayed during the national anthem. The professional competence was evident in how she discussed medical challenges in remote areas.

I pulled out a piece of paper and started writing her name: "Dr. Jasleen Kaur." Then stopped. What was I doing? She was a civilian dignitary. I was a military officer with protocols to follow and a career to protect.

*In morning light she walked to me,
Pink kurta like a prayer flag bright.
Her grace turned protocol to poetry,
My careful world dissolved from sight.

Among the veterans' proud display,
Her smile outshone each medal worn.
One look, and duty learned to pray
To beauty in the Kashmir morn.*

CHAPTER 4

"DINNER AND SURVEILLANCE"

November 21, 2013 - Evening

The transformation of Moti Mahal for the evening's ceremonial dinner was nothing short of magical. What had been a venue for formal military proceedings by day now glowed with subtle elegance under crystal chandeliers. The November chill outside made the warm interior feel like a sanctuary, amber light reflecting off polished wooden floors while regimental silver gleamed on tables draped in crisp white linen.

As the officer responsible for seating arrangements, I had spent hours ensuring that military protocol and social considerations were perfectly balanced. Each placement card had been written in elegant calligraphy and each chair was positioned with mathematical precision. What my commanding officer didn't know was the deliberate adjustment I had made to place Dr. Jasleen Kaur beside my own seat—a minor breach of protocol justified by the convenient fiction that it would allow me to address any medical concerns raised by civilian guests.

My pulse hammered as I checked the display board one final time, confirming that everything was in order. The possibility of spending an entire evening beside Jasleen sent anticipation coursing through my veins like electricity.

"Everything to your satisfaction, Lieutenant?" asked the mess Havildar Harphool Singh, interrupting my thoughts.

"Perfect, Harphool," I replied, quickly composing myself. "The mess staff has outdone themselves."

"Wait until you taste the menu, sir," he said with pride. "Five courses of regimental specialties."

The first guests began arriving promptly at 1900 hours, officers in dress uniforms escorting spouses in elegant attire, civilian dignitaries bringing diversity to the predominantly military gathering. I performed my welcoming duties with outward calm, though my eyes frequently darted to the entrance.

When she finally appeared, the sight nearly stole my breath. Dr. Jasleen Kaur stood framed in the doorway, transformed from the professional I had met earlier to an embodiment of timeless elegance. Her emerald green gown—the color of spring leaves and new beginnings—flowed gracefully to the floor, complemented by minimal jewelry that spoke of refined taste rather than ostentatious display.

Her hair, earlier pinned for the day's formalities, now cascaded in soft waves with just a delicate silver pin keeping it from obscuring her face. The overall effect was mesmerizing—bridging classical beauty with modern confidence in a way that made every other person in the room seem to fade into the background.

Professional duty compelled me forward to welcome her formally. "Dr. Kaur, welcome to Moti Mahal's evening celebration," I said, my voice thankfully steady despite the chaos in my chest.

"Thank you, Lieutenant Kumar," she replied with a smile that seemed to illuminate the space between us. "The transformation of this historic venue is quite remarkable."

"If you'll allow me," I offered, "I can show you to your place for dinner."

As we moved through the gathering, I became acutely aware of how many eyes followed our progress—some curious, some appreciative, some perhaps even envious. Dr. Kaur acknowledged greetings with gracious nods but maintained a dignified reserve that I found increasingly intriguing.

"Your seat, Doctor," I said as we reached the table, pulling out her chair with practiced formality.

"Thank you," she responded, settling into place with natural grace. "I see I'm seated beside you this evening."

"A fortunate coincidence," I replied, hoping my deliberate arrangement wasn't transparent. "I can answer any questions you might have about military traditions during dinner."

Her subtle smile suggested she might have seen through my pretense, but before she could respond, the ceremonial dinner officially began with the entrance of the regimental band. The bagpipers, in their traditional regalia, processed around the perimeter of the room, their music filling the space with stirring martial melodies.

I noticed that Jasleen was studying the menu card instead of watching this spectacle. Gathering my courage, I gently touched her arm and directed her attention to the band with a wordless gesture. The momentary contact sent an electric current through my fingertips, and I saw a similar reaction flash across her features before she composed herself and turned to watch the musicians.

The five-course military dinner unfolded with ceremonial precision. Each dish represented regimental traditions and regional specialties, accompanied by appropriate wines and punctuated by formal toasts to fallen comrades and the President of India.

I noticed that Dr. Kaur consistently selected the non-vegetarian options—a small detail that nevertheless pleased me as it mirrored my own preferences. Our conversation flowed with surprising ease, touching on her medical training, my military education, shared interests in regional history, and mutual admiration for the mountains that surrounded us.

"The mutton is particularly good," I commented as we enjoyed the main course. "It's prepared according to a recipe that dates back to the regiment's founding."

"It's excellent," she agreed. "Though I imagine field rations are somewhat less impressive."

"A significant understatement," I laughed. "Military cuisine exists on two entirely different planes—ceremonial elegance and tactical necessity."

Each exchange revealed new facets of her character—intellectual curiosity about regional politics, compassionate insights into healthcare challenges, subtle humor about military bureaucracy, and occasional glimpses of vulnerability that made her accomplishments all the more impressive.

"Tell me about your work at the district hospital," I said, genuinely curious. "It must be challenging, especially in this region."

Her expression grew thoughtful. "Every patient has a story, Lieutenant. Sometimes they're stories of hope—children recovering from illness, families reunited after accidents. Sometimes they're stories of loss—farmers who can't afford medicine, mothers who walk twenty kilometers for basic care."

"Do you treat everyone the same way?" I asked something in her tone making me probe deeper.

"A doctor's oath doesn't distinguish between Hindu and Muslim, Indian and..." she paused, seeming to choose her words carefully, "...and those who might hold different political views. Pain is pain. Suffering is suffering."

As dinner concluded and guests moved to the lawn for the cultural program, I seized the opportunity to continue our conversation in a less formal setting. The Naga regiment's bamboo dance had just begun, its rhythmic complexity capturing the attention of most attendees.

"Their coordination is remarkable," Jasleen observed as we watched the dancers navigate the clapping bamboo poles with precise footwork. "It reminds me of surgical teams—different movements but similar precision."

"An apt comparison," I replied, appreciating her professional perspective. "Both require trust, timing, and countless hours of practice."

As the evening progressed toward its conclusion, I realized with growing dismay that our time together would soon end. The thought prompted an impulsiveness unusual for my military-trained mind.

Under the pretext of offering her a tissue, I placed the paper beside her hand as she signed the guest book, our eyes meeting in a moment of unspoken communication. Her cheeks flushed slightly as she understood my intent, and without hesitation, she wrote her phone number on the tissue before sliding it discreetly back toward me.

I pocketed the precious paper immediately, aware that several observers had noticed our exchange but unable to summon appropriate concern about protocol at that moment.

Before I could suggest a quieter place for conversation, her phone rang, cutting through our moment of connection. She checked the screen, her expression shifting subtly from joy to something more complex—concern, perhaps, or tension.

She declined the call quickly, returning the phone to her evening purse. Something in her manner had changed, a subtle stiffening that hadn't been there moments before.

"Important call?" I asked gently.

"Nothing that can't wait," she replied, but I caught the slight tremor in her voice.

Before I could inquire further, she surprised me by asking for my number instead. I dialed her number from my phone, watching as her face brightened when the connection was confirmed. That simple exchange—digits flowing through space between our devices—felt like the beginning of something significant.

Our shared moment of quiet celebration was abruptly interrupted by the appearance of Major Isaac Francis, the intelligence officer whose perpetually serious demeanor seemed even more grave than usual. He carried a handheld electronic device that emitted increasingly rapid beeps as he approached our position.

The major's hand landed heavily on my shoulder, his expression grim as the device's signal peaked and a green LED began blinking steadily. Without explanation, he moved toward the Brigadier, whispering urgently while displaying the screen of his device.

The atmosphere in the garden transformed instantly. Music ceased, conversations halted, and expressions hardened into professional concern. My commanding officer was summoned to the impromptu conference, and I watched with growing unease as their gazes repeatedly turned toward Jasleen and me.

"What's happening?" Jasleen whispered, her voice steady despite the evident tension.

"I'm not certain," I replied honestly, though battlefield intuition was already suggesting possibilities—none of them reassuring.

The Brigadier approached us directly, his manner formal but his eyes conveying deeper concern. "Lieutenant Murari, a word please," he said, his tone leaving no room for delay.

As I stepped aside with him, his instructions were delivered with quiet intensity. "There appears to be a security concern, Lieutenant. I need you to ask Dr. Kaur to delete your contact information immediately, and you will do the same with hers. This is not a suggestion—it's an order."

"Sir, may I ask the nature of—" I began, but he cut me off with a sharp gesture.

"Not now, Murari. Execute the order immediately."

With a heavy heart and countless unanswered questions, I returned to Jasleen. The joy that had illuminated her features throughout the evening had been replaced by wary apprehension.

"Dr. Kaur," I began formally, conscious of the numerous eyes now watching us, "I've been instructed to request that you delete my contact information from your phone. I must do the same with yours."

Confusion and hurt flashed across her features before she turned her expression into careful neutrality. Her fingers trembled slightly as she removed her phone from her purse, each movement deliberate as she navigated to her contacts and deleted my number under the watchful gaze of senior officers.

I did the same, the simple digital action feeling paradoxically like both betrayal and duty. When it was done, we stood in awkward silence, the connection that had been building throughout the evening severed by unseen security concerns.

"I should go," she said finally, her voice barely above a whisper.

"I'm sorry," I replied, those inadequate words carrying the weight of explanations I couldn't offer and questions I wasn't permitted to ask.

She turned toward the exit without further comment, her green gown flowing gracefully around her as she departed. The color that had earlier seemed to embody springtime vitality now struck me with different symbolism—the same vibrant green that dominated the Pakistani flag against its white background.

As she disappeared from view, Major Isaac approached me directly. "Report to headquarters at 0700 tomorrow, Lieutenant," he instructed, his voice low. "This incident requires complete investigation."

That night, sleep eluded me entirely. My thoughts oscillated between memories of our conversations—each word and gesture now scrutinized for hidden meanings—and anxiety about the security implications that had prompted such dramatic intervention.

The beauty had indeed caused a battle, though not of arms and ammunition but of competing loyalties within my own heart. As dawn approached without bringing rest, one question dominated my thoughts: Who was Dr. Jasleen Kaur, and why had our simple exchange triggered such alarm among my superiors?

*In Moti Mahal's golden gleam,
Her emerald gown caught candle's fire.
Numbers passed like lovers' dream
Till signals pierced our sweet desire.

"Delete her contact," came the order,
Cold duty crushed what warmth had grown.
She walked away across night's border,
Leaving me to stand alone.*

CHAPTER 5

"THE INTERROGATION"

November 22, 2013–0700 hours

I could barely sleep that night. My mind raced with questions about what had happened and why a simple exchange of phone numbers had caused such an extreme reaction from my superiors.

The November morning was crisp and unforgiving as I walked across the parade ground toward headquarters. My breath formed small clouds in the cold air, and frost crunched under my boots with each measured step.

I woke up to a loud banging on my door at 0630 hours. It was Captain Sahil, his face tight with an urgency that made my stomach clench like a fist closing around broken glass.

"Murari, CO wants you immediately. No 1 combat dress."

My mouth went completely dry as I walked into the conference room. The space wasn't just filled with my CO—there were people from Intelligence, from Signal Interception, and Major Isaac, all waiting like predators surrounding wounded prey. My hands trembled slightly as I stood at attention, sweat already forming on my back despite the morning chill.

Almost immediately, they started firing questions at me like artillery rounds, each one calculated to break down my defenses.

"Lieutenant, when did you first meet Dr. Jasleen?" The Intelligence officer leaned forward, his voice sharp as a bayonet.

"Sir, yesterday at the Poonch Link Up Day celebration. She was representing the medical community," I replied, fighting to keep my voice steady even as my pulse pounded in my ears like distant mortar fire.

"And what exactly made you approach her?" Major Isaac cut in, his eyes narrowed with suspicion that made my uniform collar feel suddenly too tight.

"I didn't approach her, sir. She was seated at my table during dinner as per the seating plan." I felt sweat forming between my shoulder blades, my collar suddenly feeling like a noose around my throat.

"So she approached you?" the Intelligence officer pounced on my words like a predator.

"No, sir. During dinner, she was seated beside me according to protocol." My shoulders tensed as I felt the trap closing around my words, each question designed to corner me.

"Did she ask specifically about your posting? Your unit? Your responsibilities?" The questions came rapid-fire, each one making my stomach twist tighter like someone was slowly turning a screw in my gut.

"No, sir. We talked about normal things. Her work at the hospital, the ceremony, regional history—"

"Regional history?" Major Isaac interrupted, his voice dripping with suspicion. "Did she perhaps ask about troop movements? Strategic locations? Security protocols?"

"No, sir! Nothing like that." My headache grew worse with each question, a steady pounding behind my eyes like someone was using my skull for target practice.

For four hours, they questioned me. By noon, they finally let me go for lunch. My legs felt weak as I walked out, exhaustion weighing on me like a heavy pack after a twenty-kilometer march.

When I stumbled out of the room, Captain Sahil was standing right outside. "Murari, are you alright? You look like you've seen a ghost."

I gave him a look that I knew revealed everything I was feeling—confusion, indignation, fear churning together like a storm in my chest.

Then he told me the truth, and my blood turned to ice water in my veins.

"The woman you were talking to, Dr. Jasleen, is suspected of being a Pakistani Agent. She received a call from Pakistan during the function that she quickly disconnected."

The room seemed to spin around me, the floor shifting under my feet like the deck of a ship in a storm.

"WHAT? Pakistani Spy Agent?" My voice cracked like breaking glass. I couldn't believe what I was hearing. My brain refused to process the information, like a weapon jamming when you most need it to fire.

As he explained the investigation details, I felt my chest tighten until I could barely breathe, as if someone was slowly tightening a rope around my ribs. They were tracking her phone, following her movements, recording all her calls, checking bank accounts—the full surveillance package typically reserved for confirmed threats to national security.

This was my worst nightmare come to life. I had potentially compromised myself with someone suspected of espionage. My career, my oath, my very identity as a soldier—all potentially jeopardized by one evening of connection that now felt like walking through a minefield blindfolded.

"Murari, there's more," Sahil sir continued, his voice gentler now, seeing the shock on my face. "Intelligence says she has family connections across the border. Regular communication with Pakistan numbers. Money transfers that could be operational funding."

Each revelation hit me like physical blows. The woman who had seemed so genuine, so dedicated to healing—was it all an elaborate performance? Had I been played by a professional who was trained to manipulate men exactly like me?

I couldn't move. My mouth hung open in shock. Silent tears ran down my face—something that hadn't happened since my first week at the Academy when Drill Sergeant Krishnan had broken me down to rebuild me as a soldier. I turned and walked away on unsteady feet, feeling like the mountains themselves had collapsed onto my shoulders.

The cold bit through my uniform, but I barely felt it. Inside, I was burning with shame and confusion. How could I have been so wrong about someone? How could my instincts—trained through years of military education—have failed me so completely?

In my quarters, I sat on my narrow cot and stared at the wall. My hands shook as I replayed every moment of our interactions. Her laugh during the cultural program. The way she'd spoken about treating all patients equally. The gentle touch when she'd written her number on that tissue.

Was any of it real? Or was I just another target in whatever operation she was running?

The questions hammered in my head like artillery bombardment. Had she chosen me specifically because I was an artillery officer with access to sensitive information? Was the attraction I felt one-sided, manufactured by a professional who knew exactly how to make a lonely soldier fall for her lies?

Evening came, but I didn't report to the mess hall. I couldn't face my fellow officers, couldn't stomach the thought of casual conversation when my world had been turned upside down. Instead, I lay on my cot, staring at the ceiling, feeling like a fool who had endangered everything he'd sworn to protect for the sake of a beautiful face and a melodious voice.

Major Isaac appeared at my door just before lights out.

"Lieutenant, I know this is difficult," he said, his voice surprisingly gentle. "But you need to understand—this is exactly how they operate. Beautiful women, educated, dedicated to their communities. Perfect covers for intelligence operations."

His words felt like salt in an open wound.

"The phone call last night—it came from a number in Muzaffarabad. That's not a coincidence, Murari. That's operational communication."

I closed my eyes, trying to block out his words, but they kept coming like mortar rounds landing closer and closer to their target.

"Get some sleep, Lieutenant. Tomorrow we begin a deeper investigation. And Murari—" he paused at my door, "—this stays classified. One word to anyone, and you'll face court martial for security violations."

After he left, I lay in the darkness, my mind churning like a battlefield after bombardment—everything familiar was destroyed, leaving only questions and devastation. The woman I had thought might be the answer to prayers I hadn't known I was praying had turned out to be my worst nightmare.

Outside my window, the stars shone with cold indifference over Poonch, as if mocking my foolishness. What had felt like cosmic alignment just twenty-four hours ago now seemed like the cruelest joke the universe could play on a soldier who had dared to believe in something beyond duty and suspicion.

**Four hours in that sterile room,*
Questions fell like mortar rounds.
"Pakistani spy!" they spelled my doom,
Truth and lies switched battlegrounds.

My shaking hands, my breaking faith,
The love I thought divine became.
A poisoned cup, a burning wraith,
*My heart consumed in duty's flame.**

CHAPTER 6

"WINTER WATCH AT MANDI"

December 2013–February 2014

Three months passed, and I still couldn't forget Jasleen.

December brought the brutal Himalayan winter like an enemy offensive—sudden, merciless, transforming the landscape into a crystalline battlefield where every breath formed clouds and exposed skin burned with cold. I threw myself into work with an intensity that concerned even my superiors, desperate to drown out the questions that hammered in my skull like persistent artillery.

The temperature dropped so low it felt personal, and I got my first real test—relief duty at an outpost in Mandi, 37 kilometers from Poonch. Being in charge of the road opening party felt like someone had placed a physical weight on my shoulders.

I'll never forget that first morning. The darkness slowly, reluctantly gave way to dawn as I stood next to Major Ashish, the officer I was replacing. The cold was unlike anything I'd ever felt before—not just cold, but a living, angry thing that crawled into every cell of my body. My breath formed clouds in front of my face, my fingers became useless lumps around my rifle, and the metal of my weapon burned against my skin from the cold.

"Lieutenant," Major Ashish's voice seemed to come from miles away though he was right beside me. "This stretch has seen three IED incidents in the past year. The locals are a mixed basket—most supportive, some hostile. Trust your instincts, but verify everything."

I tried to nod, but my frozen neck muscles screamed in protest. His words seemed to bounce off the snow-covered pines and echo through the emptiness around us. He pointed to some houses nestled against the mountainside.

"That village lost two young men to militancy last summer. The mother of one still protests and abuses when army vehicles pass." His breath made ghost-like clouds between us. "And that ridge line? Perfect spot for observers. Never let your men linger there."

Every few minutes, he'd stop his briefing. "Repeat what I just told you, Lieutenant."

My tongue felt thick with nerves. My jaw fought against the cold as I struggled to form proper sentences. My pride demanded that I appear competent, but my body was surrendering to the Himalayan winter one frozen bit at a time.

A group of locals appeared around a bend in the road. Their faces were wrapped against the cold, but their eyes watched us with looks ranging from indifference to barely hidden hostility. Major Ashish went quiet, his hand instinctively moving to rest near his loaded AK-47.

"Maintain distance," he murmured. "Respectful but vigilant. Remember, in their eyes, we are both protectors and intruders."

As the civilians passed, I caught the eye of an elderly man. His gaze carried the tiredness of someone who'd seen too many seasons of conflict. For just a moment, something passed between us—not quite understanding, but maybe a recognition of our shared humanity despite the hostility that divided us.

My day would start at 0400 hours. By 0430, my team, along with our army dog **Darpan**, would be ready to begin operations. Those December mornings were brutal—temperatures dropping below freezing, icy winds that made my face numb and fingers stiff around my weapon despite thick gloves. Still, we kept our heads high and our eyes sharp, because any lapse in attention could mean lives lost.

Our job was to sanitize the road from any possible security threat and ensure no terrorist vehicles passed through that sector. We had to start working before sunrise, our breath forming thick clouds in the dark air as we methodically cleared the route, checking each culvert, each abandoned container, and each oddly placed stone that might hide death.

There was a natural spring—locals called it "**Chasma**"—where we could get drinking water. It was also the only place with a decent phone signal, a small mercy in our otherwise disconnected existence.

One morning in late December, while checking my phone for any messages from home, something caught my eye. A red Maruti 800 car drove by with a woman behind the wheel.

I watched closely and saw that the female driver's face was covered except for her eyes. Those eyes looked familiar—unmistakably so. My pulse quickened like machine gun fire.

I grew suspicious, my heart beating faster and harder against my ribs like someone was playing drums inside my chest. By the time I could react, the car had already passed.

I quickly signaled to my Junior Commissioned Officers at the other checkpoint to observe that vehicle. My JCO later informed me that this same car passed by at the same time every day—between 0830 and 0845 hours, without fail.

The next day, I positioned myself closer to the road. As the car passed, I moved nearer and looked at the rear-view mirror. I saw those coffee-dark eyes again, the same eyes that had haunted my dreams for months.

It was Dr Jasleen.

Finding her here was like discovering water in a desert when you're dying of thirst. I had wanted to talk to her for months, to understand what had happened, to know if the suspicions were true or if I had been poisoned against an innocent woman.

But I didn't approach her right away. Academy training took over—observe, assess, and gather intelligence before acting. I quietly followed her to see where she worked.

She stopped at a Primary Health Care Centre, Mandi—a small government hospital with whitewashed walls and a faded signboard. I followed at a distance, my heart pounding so hard I was sure she'd hear it if she came near.

I asked the village sarpanch about Dr. Jasleen and learned she lived near Chandak bridge. Following her became my daily routine, though I told myself it was surveillance, not obsession. Professional interest, not personal torment.

For weeks, the pattern remained the same. Every morning between 0830 and 0845, the red Maruti would pass our checkpoint. Sometimes I'd catch a glimpse of her through the windshield—always professional, always focused, driving with the careful precision of someone who knew she was being watched.

Then I saw something that turned my blood to ice water.

I remember that day perfectly—January 15, 2014. Even thinking about it now gives me goosebumps like spiders crawling up my spine.

At 0845 hours, as usual, Jasleen's car appeared. But something was different. Her car rushed at a higher speed than usual, kicking up dust clouds that hung in the frigid air like smoke signals.

And I didn't just see Jasleen in the car. There were two other men with her. They had long beards and wore traditional Kashmiri pherans—those long woolen robes that local men wear in winter, perfect for concealing weapons.

My throat tightened so suddenly I could barely breathe. Jasleen was already suspected of being an agent. Would this prove it? Was I witnessing her transporting militants? Every instinct in my body was screaming danger.

I grabbed my radio and ordered the checkpoint ahead to stop the vehicle immediately.

By the time I reached them, my soldier had already stopped the car and politely asked the occupants to step out. Our standard procedure kicked in—every time a suspicious vehicle was flagged, all weapons were pointed at the occupants, ready to fire. I could see Jasleen's knuckles whiten on the steering wheel. Her eyes, once bright with warmth, now showed only terror when they met mine.

We asked her three times to open her car door. But she didn't move, frozen like a deer in crosshairs.

Then we saw the back doors open.

The metallic click of safeties being disengaged echoed in the morning air, sounding unnaturally loud in the tense silence. One second of delay could have meant opening fire on the car. My finger hovered near the trigger, muscles tense, ready to respond to any threatening movement.

Two old men stepped out, both wearing traditional Kashmiri pherans. Their hands shook as they raised them slowly, the trembling of elderly men who understood exactly how close they were to death. One of them tried to explain in broken Hindi that they were patients traveling for treatment.

We insisted they all get out of the car and place any belongings on the ground.

I needed to check what was in that car. My training demanded it, even as my heart ached seeing the terror on Jasleen's face. Finally, she stepped out, her face pale as fresh snow, eyes wide with fear that cut through me like shrapnel. She stood perfectly still, only her hands trembling slightly.

I told my soldier to keep the weapons aimed on them while we searched the car. The tension was suffocating—like the air itself had become thick and hard to breathe, charged with the possibility of violence.

All we found were medical supplies—injections, medicines, a stethoscope. There was also a blood pressure machine that set off our metal detector with innocent electronic beeps.

Nothing else was in the car. We checked three times to be sure.

I looked at Jasleen. She stood there in shock, breathing quickly like someone who had just run for their life, her lips pressed tightly together to keep them from trembling. This must have felt like her worst nightmare come to life—surrounded by armed soldiers, suspected of terrorism, treated like an enemy in her own homeland.

I could do nothing. I had to do my duty.

Feeling a mix of relief and crushing guilt, I signaled my men to stand down.

She said nothing as she collected her scattered medical supplies with unsteady hands, each movement careful and deliberate, as if any sudden motion might trigger another confrontation. Slowly, she got back in her car and drove away, not looking at anyone.

That evening, I sat by the river behind our base camp, throwing stones into the dark water and watching the ripples spread until they disappeared. Each splash echoed in the silence like drops of regret.

For the first time since the investigation began, doubt crept into my mind like morning mist. Those two elderly men had been genuine patients—I could see it in their frightened faces, hear it in their broken explanations. And Jasleen's terror had seemed real, too real to be performed.

But then I remembered Major Isaac's words: "The most dangerous spies believe in their own innocence." Was her fear genuine, or was she simply that good at her craft?

The next morning at the checkpoint, Dr. Kaur's vehicle approached at the usual time. I stood at my position, but she drove through without slowing, eyes focused straight ahead like I was invisible. The deliberate avoidance cut deeper than her terror had the day before.

My men exchanged glances but continued their duties without comment. Even they could sense that something had shifted, that the routine stop-and-search had crossed a line that couldn't be uncrossed.

That evening, my sister Rajni called. Her voice, warm and familiar, seemed to come from another world—a world where love was simple and suspicion didn't poison every interaction.

"Bhaiyya, you sound different. Tired."

"Just work, Rajni. The border keeps us busy."

"It's not work," she said with the irritating accuracy of younger sisters everywhere. "It's something else. Someone else."

I couldn't answer that. How do you explain that you've fallen for someone who might be trying to destroy everything you've sworn to protect?

"Fix it," she said simply before hanging up. "Whatever it is, fix it."

But how do you fix something when you don't even know if it's broken or if it was designed to break you from the beginning?

**December winds bite through my gear,*
At Mandi post I watch and wait.
Her red car marks each morning here,
While duty guards love's frozen gate.

Those hidden eyes behind the veil
Still make my steady pulse race wild.
Though winter's breath tells death's cold tale,
*Her warmth haunts every mountain mile.**

CHAPTER 7

"THE LANGUAGE OF EYES"

March 2014

Three weeks had passed since the car search incident. The harsh winter was slowly loosening its grip on the valley, though morning frost still painted the grass silver and the mountain peaks remained wrapped in snow. Patches of muddy earth began appearing where the sun managed to penetrate, and the air carried the faint promise of spring hidden beneath its cold bite.

I stood at my checkpoint, my breath forming smaller clouds now, my gaze fixed on the bend in the road where her car would appear any minute. The daily ritual had become both torment and anticipation—a moment of connection across a divide created by duty and suspicion.

Each day, I found myself counting the minutes until 0830 hours, when the red Maruti 800 would round the curve, carrying the enigma that was Dr. Jasleen Kaur.

That morning was different. At Chasma, I noticed Dr. Jasleen's red Maruti parked on the roadside. She was approaching on foot, a steel water bottle clutched tightly in her hand. She needed water from the spring—the only source of fresh drinking water in the area, crystal clear and cold enough to make your teeth ache.

Even from a distance, the morning light caught her features in a way I hadn't noticed before. Despite the winter's harshness, her skin seemed to glow with natural radiance against the stark landscape. The cold had brought a flush to her cheeks, adding warmth to her complexion that contrasted with the clinical detachment she usually maintained.

My soldiers tensed immediately. I raised my hand, signaling my men to remain vigilant but not aggressive. Academy reflexes screamed danger—a suspicious person approaching a military checkpoint, carrying an object, deviating from established patterns.

As she drew closer, doubt crept in. Could that innocent-looking bottle contain explosives? I couldn't take chances.

"Stop right there," I commanded, my voice carrying across the clearing.

She froze, her eyes widening with recognition and fear. The color drained from her face like water flowing from a broken dam. In an instant, six assault rifles were aimed at her slender frame, the metallic clicks of safeties being disengaged breaking the morning silence.

The beauty I had glimpsed moments before was now veiled by pure dread, her delicate features tightening, her luminous eyes becoming pools of terror. Even in her fear, there was something striking about her—vulnerability transforming her loveliness into something fragile and human that made my duty suddenly feel brutal.

"Place the bottle on the ground and step back," I ordered, maintaining my professional demeanor despite the war raging in my chest.

Her hands trembled as she set the bottle down. I noticed goosebumps rising on her exposed wrists—a physiological response to extreme stress, not cold. My medical training from the Academy helped me read the signs of genuine terror. "Open it and pour out the contents," I instructed.

For a moment, she seemed unable to comprehend, her mind struggling to process commands through the fog of fear. Then, with shaking hands, she unscrewed the cap and tipped the bottle. Clear water splashed onto the frozen ground, forming a small puddle that immediately began to crystallize in the morning cold.

Something broke inside me watching her frightened compliance. The intelligence reports, the suspicions, the protocols—all necessary, all justified—but in that moment, all I could see was a human being terrified by my actions.

That evening, I sought out the village sarpanch again, a weathered man whose ancestral knowledge of local families stretched back generations.

"Dr. Jasleen?" the old man repeated, stroking his white beard. "Her family has served this region for three generations. Her grandfather treated wounded civilians during the '47 conflict, without asking which side they supported."

I listened as the sarpanch recounted stories of Jasleen's dedication—treating children in remote villages, refusing more lucrative positions in major cities, and organizing vaccination drives despite terrorist threats. Each story painted a picture of someone whose roots in this community ran deeper than any intelligence file could capture.

My covert intelligence source—a local shopkeeper—confirmed the same. "Nothing suspicious about the doctor, sahib. She lives simply, works hard, speaks kindly to everyone regardless of religion or politics."

As I walked back to my post through the starlit night, conflicting narratives battled within me. The intelligence brief marked her as a potential threat. The suspicious call from across the border. Her fearful eyes at gunpoint. The universal respect she commanded among locals.

Could the intelligence be wrong? Or was she simply that good at her cover?

The next morning brought our usual encounter. Her car appeared at precisely 0837 hours. I noticed the slight deceleration as she neared our position, the momentary pause before she presented her identification—small signs of the trauma our confrontation had caused.

But something had changed. The raw fear I had witnessed yesterday had transformed into something more complex. As she handed me her ID card, our fingers brushed momentarily, and her eyes—those expressive eyes—met mine with a questioning glance.

Days passed, each bringing our brief morning interaction. I began to notice subtle changes. She no longer averted her gaze when handing over her documents. Sometimes, a hesitant smile would flicker across her features before disappearing behind professional neutrality.

I found myself equally transformed by these daily moments. The suspicion that had once dominated my thoughts gradually receded, replaced by anticipation of our fleeting connection. I began to recognize the language her eyes spoke—anxiety giving way to cautious warmth, fear melting into something that resembled tentative trust.

"Good morning, Lieutenant," she said one day, breaking our unspoken agreement to minimize verbal interaction.

"Good morning, Doctor," I replied, surprised by the simple exchange that felt monumental in its normalcy.

As the March days grew slightly warmer and the patches of mud expanded, our silent communication evolved. A nod of acknowledgment. A genuine smile. A lingering glance. Each small gesture built an unseen bridge across the chasm of suspicion and protocol that separated us.

Then came the morning that shattered our fragile routine.

I stood at my usual position, checking my watch—0836 hours. Her car appeared, but something was wrong. She didn't slow at the checkpoint. Instead, the red Maruti accelerated past me, Jasleen's face a mask of determination, not even glancing in my direction.

Two emotions collided within my chest—concern for her unusual behavior and the resurgence of professional suspicion. Was she finally revealing her true purpose? Was she responding to some operational trigger? Or was she simply rushing to a medical emergency?

"Follow that vehicle," I ordered my driver, jumping into the jeep with my weapon ready.

We pursued her to the hospital, where she abandoned her car haphazardly near the entrance and rushed inside, still not acknowledging my presence as I approached.

Through the hospital windows, I caught glimpses of commotion—staff running, equipment being moved rapidly. Then I saw him—an elderly man in a long traditional coat, being rushed on a gurney.

As I stood outside the hospital, torn between duty and conviction, realization descended upon me. If she was innocent—truly innocent—then what had I done? For months, I had been a source of fear in her daily life. My weapons pointed at her car, my soldiers searching her belongings, my suspicion following her every move.

The thought sent a wave of shame through me like shrapnel cutting through flesh. I had terrorized an innocent woman dedicated to healing, all based on circumstantial evidence and professional paranoia. I needed to make amends—not to establish improper contact, but to ease the fear I had created.

I formulated a plan. I would visit the hospital officially, under the pretext of establishing medical support for my unit.

"Sir, we can contact headquarters for medical supplies," my junior officer suggested when I mentioned visiting the local hospital.

"No," I replied firmly. "In emergencies, we need immediate local support. We should establish contact with local medical facilities."

With my full team in protective equipment, we entered the hospital. Patients and staff parted before us like water before a ship's bow, faces registering shock at the armed soldiers suddenly filling the corridors.

"Where is the doctor?" I asked the receptionist, who pointed toward a male physician emerging from an examination room, name plate on his lab coat read Dr Suneer.

"I'm looking for the other doctor as well," I added. "The female physician."

"Dr. Jasleen is with a patient," the Dr Suneer replied, tension evident in his voice. "Perhaps I can help instead?"

I reassured him. "We're not here for any specific search or issue. We simply want to establish a good rapport with local medical resources for our unit's needs."

Relief washed over the doctor's face like a sunrise after a long night. "I can introduce you to Dr. Jasleen if you'd like to speak with both of us."

The Dr Suneer entered the examination room first, speaking softly in the local dialect. When I followed, I found Jasleen standing rigidly beside an examination table, her face pale with shock.

Outside the window, my quick reaction team stood with weapons at the ready—standard procedure for any unplanned entry into civilian buildings.

At that moment, I made a decision that defied all military protocol. I turned to my men and ordered, "QRT, move away from the windows. Stand down."

Then, with deliberate slowness, I removed my protective gear and handed my weapon to my buddy.

"I just want to talk," I said softly to Jasleen, whose eyes reflected disbelief at my vulnerability. "To make things right."

Watching her work—the gentle efficiency of her movements, the professional compassion in her voice as she reassured the frightened patient—I felt the last of my suspicions crumble like snow in the spring sunshine.

This was no spy. This was a healer.

**At Chasma spring with bottle raised,*
She faced my guns with quiet grace.
While soldiers watched and orders blazed,

Her courage lit her frightened face.

No words passed in that tense hour,
Just eyes that spoke what lips couldn't say.
Truth blooms slow, like mountain flower,
In ground where trust must find its way. *

CHAPTER 8

"ENEMY'S HEART, HEALER'S HANDS"

April 2014

The hospital courtyard had transformed into something resembling a military zone. Local police, summoned by concerned citizens who had witnessed armed soldiers entering the medical facility, established a perimeter alongside my men. From her window, Dr. Jasleen watched the surreal scene unfold—armed personnel, military vehicles, and police barricades surrounding what should have been a sanctuary of healing.

"You don't have the law in your hands," the police inspector informed me, his voice low but firm. "Whatever your suspicions, this is a civilian hospital."

I nodded, understanding the complexities. "We're not here for an operation. I'm establishing medical contact for my unit."

Before the inspector could respond, a commotion erupted at the hospital entrance. A group of villagers was carrying an elderly man who appeared to be in severe distress, his face gray as old concrete, breathing labored and shallow.

I recognized him immediately—Hashim Khan, a known government critic whose inflammatory speeches had earned him a prominent place in our intelligence files. He was suspected of supporting anti-national elements and had vocally opposed security forces at local gatherings. His history of seditious rhetoric made him a person of intense interest to our intelligence network.

Was this a medical emergency or something more sinister? A convenient cover for a meeting with a known sympathizer of insurgency? I positioned my men around the hospital perimeter, battlefield intuition and suspicions in full alert.

The coincidence seemed too perfect—Jasleen rushing past our checkpoint to meet with a man who was on our watch list. And yet, something in her urgency seemed genuine, making my growing belief in her innocence war with professional instincts.

"Heart attack!" someone shouted. "Please help!"

The medical staff sprang into action like a well-drilled military unit, but I noticed Jasleen freeze momentarily, her eyes meeting mine across the crowded room. In that split-second exchange, I saw her professional obligation warring with her fear of me. Then determination won out, and she rushed to the patient's side.

"Get the ECG machine!" Jasleen commanded, her voice transformed from the tentative tone I had heard before to one of absolute authority. This was a different woman—not the frightened suspect at checkpoints, but a medical professional in her element, radiating competence and control.

The hospital erupted into organized chaos. Nurses prepared equipment with practiced efficiency, the male doctor administered injections, and Jasleen bent over the elderly patient, her stethoscope pressed to his chest. Despite everything between us, I found myself admiring her focused professionalism.

Battlefield intuition took over, and I ordered my men to secure the area. The sniffer dog Darpan was brought in to check for explosives—standard procedure in regions where terrorist attacks on public facilities were a real threat.

"Sir, do we need to examine the patient?" one of my soldiers asked quietly.

I hesitated, protocol battling with humanity. The medical emergency appeared genuine, but my training demanded verification. This man had called us occupiers, had spoken against everything I'd sworn to protect.

"At least let us check what's under his coat," the soldier persisted.

Jasleen overheard the exchange and turned to me, her eyes blazing with righteous anger that reminded me why I'd been drawn to her in the first place.

"This man is having a myocardial infarction," she said, her voice steady despite the tension crackling around us. "If you delay his treatment for security protocols, you become responsible for his fate."

I made my decision in that moment—not as a soldier following orders, but as a human being faced with another human being's suffering. "Continue treatment, Doctor. We'll adapt our security measures accordingly."

I instructed my men to maintain a perimeter but not interfere with medical procedures. The sniffer dog completed its circuit of the room without alerting to anything suspicious—just the innocent smells of antiseptic, medicine, and human fear.

On the examination table, Hashim Khan's condition was deteriorating rapidly. The ECG machine showed alarming patterns like enemy artillery on radar, and the monitor tracking his vital signs beeped with increasing urgency that made my pulse quicken in sympathy.

"Blood pressure dropping," the nurse announced. "Oxygen saturation at 82%."

Jasleen worked with a focused intensity that reminded me of artillery crews under fire—every movement precise, every second critical. She administered medications and adjusted oxygen flow with the kind of expertise that comes from years of saving lives in impossible circumstances.

"We need to get him to a facility with cardiac care capabilities," she announced, not looking up from her patient. "He needs intervention we can't provide here."

Outside the hospital, the situation had grown more complex. Villagers had gathered, their faces etched with concern for the elder who I knew was both a former village schoolmaster and vocal critic of military presence. I recognized several faces in the crowd—people who had attended his inflammatory speeches, who had been photographed at anti-government protests. Yet here they were, genuinely concerned for his health, their whispered prayers creating an undercurrent of sound beneath the medical directives inside.

It was a stark reminder that even those we labeled as threats were human beings with communities that cared for them.

"The closest cardiac facility is in Jammu," the Dr Suneer informed me. "Seven to eight hours by road, given the current conditions."

"He won't survive that journey without life support," Jasleen added, finally looking at me directly.

I recognized the gravity of the situation. A civilian was dying—an adversarial one who had spoken against everything I stood for, who had potentially encouraged violence against forces like mine—and I had the capacity to help. My training said this man was a threat; my duty to national security suggested letting nature take its course might remove a problem. Yet my humanity rebelled at the thought.

Whatever suspicions might exist about Dr. Jasleen, whatever the patient's political alignments, this medical emergency was undeniably real. And in that moment, I had to decide what kind of officer—what kind of man—I truly was.

I made a series of rapid calls—first to the police inspector, then to the Superintendent of Police, and finally to the Director General of Police. I deliberately omitted mentioning the patient's identity in the first two calls, knowing it might complicate matters. When the DG asked directly, I had to be honest.

"It's Hashim Khan, sir," I said, bracing for the response.

There was a long pause. "The same Khan who called our forces 'occupiers' at the district meeting last month?"

"Yes, sir. The same."

Another pause. "And you're requesting emergency evacuation for this man?"

"He's a civilian in critical condition, sir," I replied, my voice steadier than I felt. "Whatever his politics, he deserves medical care."

My request was clear but professionally risky: we needed air evacuation for a civilian heart attack patient who happened to be a known critic of the government and a suspected supporter of anti-national elements.

"There's a helicopter assigned to the Vaishno Devi pilgrimage route," the DG informed me after a tense conversation. "I'll divert it to your location. ETA thirty minutes."

I turned to Jasleen, who was still working frantically to stabilize the patient. "Helicopter incoming. Thirty minutes. Can you keep him stable?"

For the first time that day, genuine relief flooded her features like sunrise breaking through storm clouds. "We'll do everything possible. Thank you, Lieutenant."

The next half hour unfolded in a blur of coordinated activity. The patient was prepared for transport, necessary medications were gathered, and a landing zone was cleared in the field adjacent to the hospital. I found myself working alongside the medical team, our previous antagonism temporarily suspended by shared purpose.

When the distinctive thump of helicopter rotors finally echoed across the valley like mechanical thunder, I saw tears of relief glistening in Jasleen's eyes. The sound that usually meant military operations now meant salvation.

Together, we supervised the loading of the patient onto the aircraft, our previous roles as suspect and interrogator temporarily forgotten. For those few minutes, we were just two people working to save a life, the most fundamental human cooperation possible.

As the helicopter lifted off, carrying Hashim Khan toward advanced medical care in Jammu, I watched it shrink against the vast Himalayan sky. In that moment, something fundamental shifted in my understanding. The complexity of our situation—military duty, security concerns, human connection—couldn't be reduced to simple categories of suspicion and trust.

Standing there in the swirling dust of the helicopter's departure, I realized we had found common ground in the most unexpected place. Not in romance or rebellion against protocol, but in the shared commitment to preserving life amidst circumstances that threatened to extinguish it.

As the crowd began to disperse and normal hospital operations resumed, Jasleen approached me. Her professional facade had softened, and for the first time since that night at the ceremonial dinner, I saw genuine warmth in her eyes.

"Thank you," she said simply. "For choosing to see him as a patient, not just a name in a file."

"Every life has value," I replied, surprised by my own words. "Even when politics tries to convince us otherwise."

She nodded, then did something unexpected—she smiled. Not the cautious, professional expression I'd grown accustomed to, but a real smile that transformed her entire face and reminded me why I'd been drawn to her from that first morning.

"Perhaps," she said quietly, "there's more humanity in soldiers than people realize."

As I walked back to my vehicle, I felt lighter than I had in months. The spring air carried the scent of apple blossoms and new possibilities. Whatever questions remained about Dr. Jasleen Kaur, whatever complexities still shadowed our situation, today had proven something important: when faced with a choice between duty and compassion, we had both chosen compassion.

It was a small beginning—a professional acknowledgment that might open the door to something more. Whether that future would bring further clarity or complication remained to be seen, but for now, it was enough to know that in at least one battle of the heart, humanity had prevailed.

**Old Hashim fell, his heart gave way,*
While I held grudges, she held life.
Her healing hands that April day
Cut through my world of war and strife.

"Send helicopter!" came my call
To save the man who cursed our name.
In mercy's choice I glimpsed it all—
*Her doctor's heart, beyond all blame.**

❀ ❀ ❀

CHAPTER 9

"MEDICINE FOR THE HEART"

April–May 2014

The weeks following Hashim Khan's evacuation brought unexpected changes to my routine. Spring had settled into the valley with full confidence now—apple orchards heavy with fruit, wildflowers painting the meadows in brilliant colors, and temperatures climbing to a pleasant 18–25°C that made even checkpoint duty bearable.

I returned to my quarters after the helicopter incident feeling something I hadn't experienced in months: peace. My body ached with exhaustion, but my mind felt clearer than it had since that cursed night at the ceremonial dinner. The radio at my belt buzzed—my sister Rajni responding to my brief message about the day's events.

Her reply was typically direct: "Good. Now fix the rest."

Three days later, news came through official channels that Hashim Khan's angioplasty had been successful. The old man would live, would return to his family, and would probably continue his speeches criticizing our presence. But he would be alive to do so.

I felt a weight lift from my chest that I hadn't realized was there.

Yet doubts still gnawed at me like persistent artillery fire in the distance. The Intelligence file on Jasleen contained too many red flags to ignore completely. And now her connection to Hashim Khan—treating him, rushing to save him, showing such genuine concern for a man our intelligence marked as potentially dangerous.

Was I being manipulated by feelings I couldn't control? Was her medical dedication merely the perfect cover for something more sinister?

But every time these thoughts surfaced, I remembered the way she'd worked to save his life, the tears of relief when the helicopter arrived, the genuine warmth in her smile afterward. Either she was the most accomplished actress I'd ever encountered, or she was exactly what she appeared to be—a dedicated healer caught in circumstances beyond her control.

A week later, I found myself outside the hospital again. The building seemed different now—less a potential security threat and more a place of healing where two people had found common ground. The morning air carried the scent of jasmine from a nearby garden, mixing with the clinical smell of antiseptic from open windows.

I pushed open the doors, my AK-47 slung across my shoulder—a habit born of caution I couldn't yet abandon, though it felt heavier now, more intrusive in this place dedicated to preserving life.

The staff greeted me with smiles that seemed genuine—a dramatic change from the cowering fear of my previous visits. A nurse approached with obvious warmth.

"Lieutenant sahib, welcome back," she said, her voice carrying none of the previous tension. "Everyone is still talking about what you did for Hashim chacha."

My throat tightened at the casual affection in her voice— "chacha," uncle, the term of respect that transformed a suspected threat into a beloved community elder. "Just doing what needed to be done."

"The doctor is in her office," the nurse offered without my having to ask.

I nodded my thanks and made my way down the corridor. Each step felt heavier than the last, not from physical weight but from the growing realization that I was about to cross another line—moving from professional necessity to something dangerously close to personal interest.

The door to her office was partially open. I knocked softly.

"Come in," came her voice—that melodious sound that had haunted my thoughts for months.

She was sitting at her desk, writing in a patient file, her hair pulled back in a simple ponytail that made her look younger and more approachable. When she looked up and saw me, her pen stopped moving, and for a heartbeat, we just stared at each other.

Her eyes were no longer rimmed with the red exhaustion I'd seen during the emergency, but they still carried a wariness that cut through me like shrapnel. Even in the soft light of her office, she was breathtakingly beautiful—the kind of beauty that made men forget their duty, a dangerous thought I tried to push aside.

"Lieutenant," she said, her voice carefully neutral.

"Dr. Kaur," I replied, my voice sounding strange to my own ears. I shifted my rifle to a more comfortable position, suddenly acutely aware of its weight and what it represented between us.

She set down her pen and folded her hands on the desk. "What brings you back to our hospital? Another security concern?"

The slight edge in her words was justified, but I could sense something else beneath them—curiosity, perhaps even hope.

"I wanted to check on Hashim Khan's condition," I said, falling back on the safe excuse. "And to establish better coordination between our medical needs and your facility."

"He's stable. The cardiologists in Jammu are monitoring him closely, but the prognosis is good." She paused, studying my face with the clinical attention of someone trained to read symptoms. "He would have died without your intervention."

The silence that followed felt electric. I watched her eyes soften slightly, some of the professional distance melting away like snow in spring sunshine.

"Dr. Kaur... Jasleen," I began, her name feeling intimate on my tongue. "I need to apologize for how I've treated you these past months."

"Do you know what it's like?" she interrupted, her voice barely above a whisper but carrying the weight of months of suppressed pain. "To be treated as the enemy in your own home? To have guns pointed at you while you're just trying to get water? To feel your hands shake every time you drive past a checkpoint?"

My eyes dropped to her hands, which were trembling even now as she spoke. Not the steady hands of a surgeon, but hands made unsteady by fear—fear that I had caused.

"I have nightmares," she continued, her voice breaking slightly. "In them, I'm always trying to help someone, to save someone, but there's always a gun pointed at me. Always a voice telling me to stop."

I stood there, absorbing her words like physical blows, each one deserved and devastating.

"I'm sorry," I said finally, those inadequate words hanging in the air between us like smoke. "I was following protocols, but I was wrong about how I treated you personally."

Her eyes met mine, searching for something—sincerity? Understanding? Forgiveness?

Suddenly, I felt lightheaded. The room seemed to spin slightly, and I reached out to steady myself against the edge of her desk. The emotional weight of the conversation, combined with months of stress and irregular eating, was taking its toll.

Jasleen noticed immediately, her doctor's instincts overriding everything else. She rose from her chair, professional concern replacing the guarded expression on her face.

"Lieutenant, are you alright?" she asked, moving around the desk with fluid grace.

I nodded, embarrassed. "Just a bit... dizzy. Probably nothing serious."

Her eyes narrowed, assessing me with the same clinical attention she'd given Hashim Khan. Without hesitation, she pressed her fingers to my wrist, taking my pulse. The gentle pressure of her fingertips against my skin sent electricity through me that had nothing to do with my dizziness.

"Your pulse is elevated," she observed, her professional tone not quite hiding her concern. "When did you last eat a proper meal? And I mean proper—not field rations or whatever passes for food in your mess hall."

"I... don't remember," I admitted, realizing I'd been too focused on duty to consider such basic needs.

A small smile touched her lips—the first genuine one I'd seen directed at me in months, transforming her entire face. "An acute case of neglecting yourself while worrying about everyone else," she diagnosed with gentle teasing. "Combined with what I suspect is a chronic condition of putting duty before self-care."

She reached for her phone, speaking quickly in Kashmiri to someone—probably asking for tea and food to be brought. Then she guided me to a chair with the same gentle authority she'd shown with her patients.

"Sit. Let me check your blood pressure."

I obeyed, lowering myself into the chair across from her desk. She returned with a stethoscope and blood pressure cuff, her movements were professional but somehow intimate in the small space of her office.

"I'm fine, really," I protested weakly.

She ignored me, wrapping the cuff around my arm. Her face was close to mine as she listened through the stethoscope, her brow furrowed in concentration. I could see the individual eyelashes casting tiny shadows on her cheeks, could smell the subtle hint of jasmine in her hair that seemed to be her natural scent.

"120 over 80," she announced, removing the cuff. "Normal, but you're clearly exhausted. Any other symptoms? Headache? Chest tightness?"

I hesitated, then decided to seize the opportunity her professional concern had presented.

"Actually, I've been having some... discomfort," I said, desperately thinking of what ailment might require multiple follow-up visits.

"What kind of discomfort?" she asked, settling back into her chair with genuine interest.

"It's... difficult to describe." I ran a hand through my hair, feigning embarrassment. "Sometimes headaches, sometimes body aches. It comes and goes unpredictably."

She studied me for a moment, and I had the distinct impression she saw right through my vague symptoms. Then, unexpectedly, her lips twitched with what might have been amusement.

"I see. And how long has this... mysterious condition... been affecting you?"

"A few months," I lied, maintaining eye contact. "I thought it would pass on its own."

"Hmm." She picked up her prescription pad, her expression professionally serious but with something playful dancing in her eyes. "I suppose I should prescribe something for these... symptoms."

"Something effective," I suggested hopefully. "Maybe something... blue?"

Her pen paused over the prescription pad. She looked up at me with frank amusement now, no longer pretending to take my fictitious ailment seriously.

"Blue?" she repeated, one eyebrow raised. "Lieutenant Kumar, are you asking me to prescribe medicine based on color rather than therapeutic value?"

I felt my own lips curve into a smile—the first genuinely relaxed expression I'd worn in her presence. "I trust your medical expertise completely, Doctor. But if you happen to have something in blue..."

She laughed then—a genuine, delighted sound that filled the small office and seemed to dissolve months of tension between us. The sound was like music, like temple bells, like everything beautiful I'd been missing in my regimented military life.

"I'm afraid my pharmacy doesn't stock medications by color preference," she said, still smiling as she wrote on the pad. "Would pink be acceptable? Or perhaps yellow?"

"Pink would be... acceptable," I replied, enjoying the absurdity of our conversation.

She tore the prescription from the pad and handed it to me. Our fingers brushed as I took it, and neither of us pulled away immediately. The contact lingered, warm and electric, a point of connection in the cool air of her office.

I looked down at the prescription. She had indeed prescribed a mild pain reliever—nothing special medically, but at the bottom of the paper, she had drawn a small heart.

When I looked up, her expression had changed again—more vulnerable now, but with something else in her eyes that made my pulse quicken like rapid artillery fire.

A knock at the door interrupted the moment. A nurse entered with a tray—steaming tea in delicate glasses and what looked like homemade biscuits. The interruption felt both welcome and frustrating.

"Thank you, Rashida," Jasleen said to the nurse, who smiled knowingly before leaving us alone again.

She poured tea for both of us, the familiar ritual somehow making the small office feel domestic, intimate. The tea was perfect—strong, sweet, flavored with cardamom and something else I couldn't identify.

"Kehwa," she explained, noticing my expression. "Traditional Kashmiri tea. My grandmother's recipe."

I sipped the fragrant brew, feeling warmth spread through my chest that had nothing to do with the temperature of the liquid. "It's excellent. Much better than military chai."

"Everything's better when made with care instead of just efficiency," she observed quietly.

The comment seemed to carry a deeper meaning, and we sat in comfortable silence for a moment, sipping tea and pretending the world outside her office didn't exist.

"I should go," I said reluctantly, standing as I finished the tea. "But I wanted you to know that things will be different now."

She smiled at that—soft, genuine, transformative. "I'd like that, Lieutenant. Very much."

As I stepped outside the hospital into the warm spring afternoon, I felt lighter than I had in months. The prescription with its small drawn heart was folded carefully in my pocket, and the taste of kehwa lingered on my tongue like a promise of something sweeter than duty and protocol.

Whatever complications lay ahead, whatever questions remained unanswered about Dr. Jasleen Kaur's past and connections, today had proven something important: when two people choose understanding over suspicion, small miracles become possible.

The evening air carried the scent of apple blossoms and new beginnings as I walked back to base, whistling softly—something I hadn't done since before that night when everything changed.

**I came with guilt like shrapnel deep,*
Her gentle hands checked pulse and breath.
"Blue medicine?" she laughed to keep,
Our moment safe from war and death.

Her kehwa warmed what cold had froze,
While drawing hearts upon my chart.
Like spring that melts Himalayan snows,
*Her care began to heal my heart.**

CHAPTER 10

"THE GREEN APPLE"

May–June 2014

The May heat had arrived with a vengeance, transforming the morning checkpoint routines into endurance tests. Temperatures soared to 28–36°C by midday, making our protective gear feel like portable ovens. Sweat pooled beneath my kevlar vest, and the metal of my rifle grew too hot to touch without gloves.

The meeting with Major Isaac lasted longer than expected. I sat in his air-conditioned office, grateful for the relief from the blazing sun outside, while he reviewed my recent activities with the surgical precision of a man trained to find patterns in chaos.

"Your actions were unorthodox, Lieutenant," he concluded, studying me across his desk cluttered with intelligence reports. "Diverting a helicopter, involving yourself personally with a civilian previously flagged for security concerns..."

I prepared myself for disciplinary action, my shirt already damp with nervous sweat despite the cool air.

"But," he continued, surprising me, "your judgment in a critical situation saved a civilian life. The DG of Police has personally expressed his appreciation for your humanitarian approach."

My surprise must have shown on my face, because Major Isaac's expression softened fractionally—a rare crack in his professional armor.

"That said, Lieutenant Murari," he continued, his voice hardening again, "the investigation regarding Dr. Kaur is ongoing and intensifying."

"Sir?" I asked, tension coiling in my muscles like a spring under pressure.

He opened a file that made my stomach drop. I caught glimpses of surveillance photographs—high-resolution images of Jasleen at various locations around Poonch. But one photograph made my blood freeze: Jasleen at the Chakan-da-bagh gate, the crossing point to Pakistan.

"She makes regular visits to the border crossing," Major Isaac said, his voice carrying the weight of accumulated suspicion. His fingers traced the photograph as he spoke.

"We've documented six such visits in the past three months. She claims they're merely social calls, but we've never properly verified the nature of these meetings."

The photograph showed Jasleen handing a package to a middle-aged man on the Pakistani side of the gate. The package was wrapped in ordinary brown paper, its contents impossible to identify from the image.

"We've logged additional exchanges," he continued, producing more photographs. "Money transfers, small packages, extended conversations with individuals whose backgrounds we cannot verify."

"Her association with Hashim Khan adds another layer of concern," he said, showing me a photograph of Jasleen and Khan in what appeared to be a private conversation outside the hospital. "His documented ties to several anti-national groups make any connection to him potentially significant."

"He was having a heart attack," I pointed out. "She's a doctor."

"Yes, and she may well be exactly what she appears to be—a dedicated physician with unfortunate political associations." He closed the file with a decisive snap. "But we've intercepted communications suggesting otherwise, Murari. This region is too sensitive for assumptions."

He leaned forward, his voice dropping to almost a whisper. "I've seen good men lose their objectivity where beautiful women are concerned. The fact that she saved a government critic's life doesn't necessarily prove innocence—it could just as easily demonstrate the depth of her cover."

My face heated despite the air conditioning. Had I been that transparent?

"That said," he continued, "your initiative saved a life, regardless of the political implications. That counts for something."

"Thank you, sir."

"You're dismissed. Return to your checkpoint duties at Mandi. But Murari—" his voice stopped me as I turned to leave, "—maintain a professional distance. That's an order."

"Yes, sir."

I saluted and left, my mind whirling with implications. The photographs, the border meetings, the packages—each new piece of information seemed to add weight to the intelligence assessment. Yet something in my gut rebelled against accepting it completely.

The next morning, I resumed my position at the checkpoint near Chasma spring. The May sun was already brutal at 0800 hours, turning the asphalt soft and making the air shimmer with heat waves. My men went about their duties with the practiced efficiency of soldiers who had learned to work despite discomfort.

At 0843 hours—yes, I was still timing her appearances—the familiar red Maruti rounded the bend. She was driving slower than usual, and I could see her clearly through the windshield, no longer covering her face, her expression calm and professional.

When she saw me step forward to conduct the routine check, something changed in her posture. Instead of the wary tension I'd grown accustomed to, there was something that might have been a relief, even anticipation.

"Good morning, Lieutenant," she said as she rolled down her window, her voice carrying a warmth that made the oppressive heat somehow more bearable.

"Good morning, Doctor," I replied, stepping closer to her car. "Documents, please."

As she handed me her identification, our fingers brushed—a contact that lasted perhaps a second longer than necessary. The brief touch sent familiar electricity up my arm, a sensation that seemed amplified by the growing heat of the day.

"All clear today," I said, returning her papers. "You can proceed."

Instead of immediately driving on, however, she hesitated. Then, reaching beside her seat, she picked up something and held it out to me through the window.

A green apple.

The fruit was perfect—bright emerald skin that seemed to glow in the harsh sunlight, the exact shade of new leaves in spring. But as I stared at it, my mind made an unwelcome connection: the same vibrant green that dominated the Pakistani flag, the color that flew over enemy positions just a few kilometers away.

Every alarm bell in my training started ringing. Accepting gifts from civilians, especially one still under investigation, violated multiple protocols. My superiors would see this as confirmation of inappropriate contact, possibly evidence of compromise. Major Isaac's warning echoed in my mind: "Maintain professional distance. That's an order."

Yet as I looked at Jasleen's face, I saw something that made my carefully constructed suspicions waver. There was vulnerability in her expression, a hesitant hopefulness that reminded me of a child offering a drawing to a stern teacher, uncertain whether it would be accepted or rejected.

"Thank you," I said, my voice embarrassingly husky as I accepted the apple.

She didn't reply, but her eyes held mine for a moment longer than necessary. In those dark depths, I saw something complex—gratitude, certainly, but also something that might have been affection, or might have been calculation. The heat made everything shimmer, including my ability to read her true intentions.

With a small nod, she rolled up her window and drove on, leaving me standing in the blazing sun with a green apple in my hand and a thousand questions in my mind.

I stood there for a moment, the apple warm from her touch and the heat, feeling its weight both literally and symbolically. One of my men approached cautiously.

"Sir? Should we examine that?" he asked, nodding at the fruit with professional concern.

Protocol demanded yes. All items from suspect sources should be thoroughly inspected. But standing there in the scorching heat, holding something she had chosen to give me personally, I felt torn between duty and the growing certainty that this was exactly what it appeared to be—a simple gift from someone trying to bridge the gap between us.

"Check it," I said reluctantly, though every instinct rebelled against treating her kindness with suspicion.

My subordinate took the apple with professional care, conducting a thorough examination for unusual weight distribution, cuts in the skin, or any signs of tampering. After several minutes of careful inspection, he cut it in half with his field knife.

Nothing but white flesh and a small constellation of dark seeds at its core. Perfectly innocent, perfectly normal. Just an apple that happened to be green.

Yet as I watched him return the two halves to me, I couldn't shake the symbolic weight of that color choice. In this region where every gesture carried potential meaning, where green flags flew over enemy positions and green scarves marked political affiliations, could this simple gift be as innocent as it appeared?

I put the apple halves in my pocket, unable to throw away her gift despite every protocol that demanded I do exactly that. The fruit's weight against my leg felt like carrying a secret, a small rebellion against the machinery of suspicion that governed our interactions.

Five minutes later, my radio crackled with a familiar voice. Major Isaac, calling at exactly the wrong moment.

"Lieutenant Murari, status report."

"All clear, sir. Routine checkpoint operations proceeding normally."

There was a pause that seemed to stretch longer than the pause should have. Did he know about the apple? Were we under surveillance even here?

"Any unusual incidents to report?" The question felt loaded and specific.

I hesitated for a heartbeat—the space between honesty and self-preservation, between duty and the growing certainty that some things were too small and too human to fit into intelligence reports.

"Nothing significant, sir."

"Very well. Continue your duties."

As I signed off, I realized I had just lied to a superior officer for the first time in my military career. The apple halves seemed to burn against my leg like evidence of my compromised loyalties.

That evening, alone in my quarters, I sat on my narrow cot and examined the apple pieces in the light of my desk lamp. Cut cleanly in half, they revealed their simple truth—just fruit, nothing more. The seeds were arranged in the natural star pattern that every apple contained, with no hidden messages or concealed devices.

But questions multiplied in my mind like artillery calculations. Why green? Why this apple, at this time, from someone whose every action was being scrutinized for hidden meaning? Was it coincidence, or was I missing something that trained intelligence analysts would immediately recognize?

I ate one half slowly, tasting the sweet-tart flavor that reminded me of childhood orchards and simpler times when an apple was just an apple. The other half I wrapped carefully and placed in my field desk, though I couldn't have explained why.

Sleep came fitfully that night, filled with dreams of green flags and green eyes, of hands passing fruits across barbed wire while searchlights swept the darkness looking for infiltrators and spies.

I woke before dawn with the growing certainty that Dr. Jasleen Kaur was either exactly what she appeared to be—a compassionate healer trying to build bridges in a divided world—or she was the most sophisticated intelligence operative I had ever encountered.

Either way, the green apple had changed something between us, had moved us from the safe ground of professional interaction into territory where every gesture carried weight and every kindness might be a weapon.

The question that haunted me as I prepared for another day of checkpoint duty was simple and terrifying: Was I falling in love with an angel or walking into the most dangerous trap of my life?

**She handed me that emerald gift,*
While duty screamed and heart stayed mute.
Green like the hope that makes souls drift,
Green like the flag of our dispute.

My men examined every part,
Found only seeds and morning dew.
One apple couldn't hide a heart—
*But could it hide what no one knew?**

CHAPTER 11

"HIDDEN DANGERS, ALONG SACRED ROUTES"

July 25, 2014

The pre-monsoon heat was suffocating—36°C with humidity that made every uniform stick to the skin like a second layer of sweat-soaked cotton. The air hung thick and motionless, while promising rain that refused to come.

My field radio crackled with an unexpected call. I placed the handset against my ear, listening intently as my commanding officer requested my immediate presence. A nod was my only acknowledgment as I pocketed my notebook and strode toward the operations room, sweat already beading on my forehead despite the early hour.

My Commanding Officer handed me a sealed envelope from Brigade Headquarters. The official letterhead felt crisp and important in my damp hands as I broke the seal and read the orders appointing me, Lieutenant Murari, as ground security coordinator for the Buda Amarnath Yatra.

I spread the detailed maps across the table, their paper edges already wilting in the humidity despite the air conditioning. Studying the pilgrim route from Poonch to Mandi Hills, I marked choke points with red pins, sweep zones with blue, and placed green markers at proposed checkpoints. My index finger traced the mountain ridges where special forces would establish observation posts, each position calculated for maximum coverage despite the heat haze that would affect visibility.

The Yatra would pass through three sectors under my coordination: Alpha, Bravo, and Charlie. I designated additional security forces for the final days when the Chari Yatra would join the main pilgrimage—the sacred mace procession that would draw thousands of additional devotees despite the oppressive weather.

The Dasnami Akhara sadhus required special consideration for their traditional procession. These orange-robed ascetics, followers of ancient monastic orders, would carry the silver-decorated mace from Poonch to the temple amid chants and religious fervor. My security plan needed provisions for this procession while ensuring they wouldn't be hampered by obvious military presence in the crushing heat.

Every year, thousands of devotees embarked on the Budha Amarnath Yatra, a sacred pilgrimage culminating at the temple where devotees believed Lord Shiva had narrated the secrets of immortality. The journey was marked by devotion and the rhythmic beats of drums as pilgrims crossed the sacred Pulsta River, named after Rishi Pulsta. The temple's four doors, open to all directions, symbolized inclusivity—welcoming people regardless of their background, though the heat would test everyone's endurance.

At dawn, I positioned myself at the forward command post. Three army trucks converted into signal jamming and detection vehicles were parked nearby, their electronic equipment already straining against the heat. I inspected each vehicle, running my hand along sophisticated antenna arrays that would need constant cooling to function in these conditions.

With crisp verbal directions to the operators—I directed two vehicles to flank the pilgrim convoy while the third would patrol the route perimeter, creating an electronic security dome over the entire procession despite the atmospheric interference the humidity would cause.

My own command vehicle was equipped with communications equipment and a raised observation platform that would become an oven by midday. Unlike static checkpoints, I would be mobile—moving fore and aft along the pilgrim route as security needs dictated, though the heat would make rapid deployment challenging.

The Jammu & Kashmir Police Superintendent arrived with four constables, all looking wilted despite the early hour. Their body language—stiff shoulders and minimal eye contact—betrayed reluctance at being placed under a junior Army officer's coordination, compounded by irritation at working in such oppressive conditions.

I unfolded the operational chart on the hood of a jeep, pointing to sectors with economic movements while sweat dripped onto the paper. When the Superintendent began to object about jurisdiction, I simply tapped the joint operation order bearing the DIG's signature. The police officers exchanged glances but nodded, too tired from the heat to argue extensively.

By midmorning, I had established the joint command post under a large canvas awning that provided minimal relief from the blazing sun. Representatives from Army,

J&K Police, and paramilitary forces gathered, all seeking whatever shade was available. I assigned sectors through written orders, minimizing verbal communication.

A senior sadhu from Dasnami Akhara arrived unexpectedly, his saffron robes surprisingly fresh despite the heat. I welcomed him with a respectful namaste, noting how he seemed unaffected by the temperature—perhaps accustomed to such extremes through years of spiritual discipline. He had come to discuss the route for the sacred Chari mace procession.

Without words—I showed him the dedicated pathway I had planned, taking into account the need for shade stations and water distribution points. His beard-framed smile indicated approval, a crucial alliance secured despite the challenging environmental conditions.

Intelligence Bureau officers arrived at 1100 hours, their vehicles' air conditioning running continuously. They carried satellite imagery and signal intelligence reports in sealed, climate-controlled containers. I directed them to the secure briefing area—the only fully air-conditioned space available—with a subtle hand gesture.

The reports indicated suspected militant movement in the western ridges, though the heat would affect both friendly and enemy operations equally. I absorbed this information, then modified patrol patterns on my map, strengthening coverage in three vulnerable sectors while considering how the extreme temperatures would impact response times.

My soldiers understood my field signals.

The convoy of pilgrims would depart Poonch in two days. I observed the departure preparations from my command vehicle. My binoculars felt burning hot against my face as I scanned approach routes, while my radio operator constantly wiped sweat from his equipment to prevent short circuits.

Throughout the day, I adjusted my vehicle's position constantly—sometimes moving ahead to scout routes, other times falling back to observe rear security. The metal surfaces of our vehicles became untouchable by midday, requiring constant relocation to whatever shade was available.

The police officers witnessed this continuous adaptation to challenging conditions. By the third checkpoint, their initial resistance had been replaced by grudging respect for the systematic approach that accounted for environmental factors. When I indicated formation changes with quick hand movements—they complied without hesitation.

A message arrived from Brigade through secure channels: medical support teams would establish three camps along the route, with the main medical facility situated at the temple itself. The extreme heat would make medical support critical, as heat exhaustion and dehydration would be constant threats.

Dr. Kaur would be heading the temple medical facility.

My expression remained unchanged as I acknowledged the information with a single nod, though the oppressive heat seemed to intensify momentarily. I consulted my map again, marking the medical camp locations with white pins, circling the temple location twice while considering the implications.

Seven days of operations ahead, with Dr. Jasleen at the final destination point where I would need to maintain the highest security vigilance despite the personal complications her presence would create.

I added a final note to my security schedule—the timing of the Dasnami Akhara's Chari Yatra procession would coincide with the busiest day of the pilgrim movement, all during the hottest part of the summer. The sacred mace would require a dedicated security corridor without appearing to be under military protection, while temperatures would likely reach dangerous levels that could affect both pilgrims and security personnel.

An Intelligence Bureau officer approached with a file, sweat staining his shirt despite the brief walk from his air-conditioned vehicle. "Threat assessment update, sir," he said quietly. "Heat-related incidents expected to increase, along with potential for exploitation by hostile elements."

I received the file, then hesitated. My pen hovered over my notepad before writing: "Background verification request: Dr. Kaur, Civil Medical Officer. Priority assessment given upcoming operational proximity." I passed the note back without expression.

The IB officer raised an eyebrow but tucked the note into his pocket with a nod.

By sunset—the first relief from the punishing heat in twelve hours—the first day's preparation had been completed without major incident. The police superintendent approached me at the command post, his uniform finally beginning to dry in the cooling air.

"Your security grid is comprehensive," he acknowledged, the earlier resistance absent from his voice. "Accounting for environmental factors shows good planning."

I responded with a short nod, turning my attention to tomorrow's preparations while the blessed evening breeze finally provided some relief from the day's torture.

The yatra would continue for six more days of preparation, then seven operational days. Every morning, I would rise before dawn to review overnight intelligence, adjust deployments, and inspect equipment that constantly threatened to fail in oppressive conditions. Every evening, I would receive situation reports from all sectors, modifying the next day's security pattern while fighting exhaustion from the brutal temperatures.

When the Intelligence Bureau report on Dr. Kaur appeared on my desk two days later, sealed and marked confidential, I felt a moment of uncharacteristic hesitation before opening it.

Maps spread like prayers before my eyes,
Each pin a life I'm sworn to shield.
Budha Amarnath's sacred prize
Draws pilgrims to this hallowed field.

They say she'll lead the medical team
Where devotees seek divine grace.
Seven days to guard what I esteem—
Her safety in this holy place. *

CHAPTER 12

"THE YATRA – PILGRIMAGE OF HEARTS"

August 4–10, 2014 – The Seven Days

The first day of the Buda Amarnath Yatra dawned with temperatures already climbing toward 32°C at 0600 hours. By midday, the thermometer would touch 40°C, turning our security operations into an endurance test that challenged both equipment and human limits.

I positioned myself at the Alpha checkpoint, my uniform already damp with sweat despite the early hour. The signal-jamming vehicle hummed nearby, its cooling fans working overtime to prevent electronic equipment from overheating in the blazing sun. My radio operator constantly wiped moisture from his gear.

My radio crackled: convoy approaching. I acknowledged with a single downward finger gesture.

The medical vehicle appeared first through the heat haze, slowing at the checkpoint like a mirage materializing. Dr. Kaur sat behind the wheel, her white lamb coat somehow remaining crisp despite the oppressive conditions. Even through the shimmering air, I could see her professional composure intact.

The convoy continued toward the temple where Dr. Kaur would establish the main medical camp. I shifted my vehicle to the convoy's rear flank, observing the last pilgrims pass safely through a vulnerable stretch. The heat made everything shimmer like water, turning routine observation into a visual challenge. Once clear, I accelerated past the entire procession, taking a mountain shortcut to arrive at the temple grounds before the first pilgrims—standard advance security protocol.

My soldiers moved with practiced efficiency despite the heat, placing sensors and establishing observation posts without verbal commands. Sweat poured down their faces, but they maintained professional discipline even as equipment grew too hot to touch without gloves.

From my position, I observed Dr. Kaur organizing medical supplies at the temple grounds. She directed her staff with confident efficiency, establishing triage areas and medicine distribution points while ensuring proper shade for both patients and medical equipment. When our eyes briefly met across the camp, we both quickly looked away—maintaining professional distance despite the personal history between us.

The afternoon situation report indicated normal operations despite the challenging conditions. I signed the document and handed it to my runner, the paper already damp with perspiration. As the soldier departed, I prepared my vehicle to patrol the middle sector of the route where heat mirages were affecting visibility.

Before I could leave, Dr. Kaur approached, carrying an insulated container that looked impossibly fresh in the wilting heat.

"Kashmiri Kheer for the security team," she said simply, placing the container on my vehicle's hood that was already too hot to touch. "It's kept cool with ice packs." Then she turned and walked back to the medical tent without waiting for acknowledgment, her professional manner giving nothing away.

I opened the container, noting how carefully the sweet had been prepared and preserved against the heat. Ice packs surrounded smaller containers, maintaining temperature in conditions that would normally spoil food within hours. I signaled to my second-in-command, who distributed portions to the team while I studied the patrol route map, trying to ignore how the thoughtful preparation showed genuine concern for our welfare.

Within minutes, I was back in my vehicle, moving to the rear of the pilgrim column where intelligence had flagged potential concerns. The air conditioning in our vehicles was fighting a losing battle against the heat, making every patrol an endurance exercise.

This pattern repeated over the following days. I would return to the temple area after route patrols to find food near my vehicle—sometimes paratha wrapped in cooling cloths, sometimes fruit preserved in ice—always delivered by Dr. Kaur without ceremony. The offerings were shared among the security team, though I noticed my portion was always carefully separated in its own container.

My mobility along the pilgrim route became increasingly important as the heat affected both pilgrims and security personnel. When a suspicious vehicle was spotted near the second rest area, I arrived within minutes despite the challenging conditions to personally supervise the inspection. When concerns arose about heat exhaustion among elderly pilgrims at a narrow passage, I repositioned to coordinate medical support and crowd flow.

Each night, I would return to the temple base to assess the day's operations and prepare for the next, inevitably encountering Dr. Kaur as she attended to pilgrims suffering. The medical tent had become a constant hub of activity as the temperature took its toll on devotees unaccustomed to such extreme conditions.

On the third day, while reviewing patrol reports in whatever shade I could find, I received a visit from two Intelligence Bureau officers. They presented their findings on recent surveillance, then paused before addressing a secondary matter.

"About your inquiry, sir," the senior officer said quietly, wiping sweat from his forehead. "We've completed the background verification on Dr. Kaur. Nothing irregular in her profile or recent communications."

I acknowledged with a nod, my expression unchanged despite the relief that washed over me like a cooling breeze. The officers departed quickly, seeking the comfort of their air-conditioned vehicles.

That evening, as my vehicle returned from patrolling the outer perimeter through the air that felt like breathing from an oven, two of Dr. Kaur's medical staff approached me with urgent gestures. They pointed toward the water storage area where something required my attention.

I followed at a measured pace, hand resting near my sidearm. As we rounded the supply tents, I spotted the K-9 unit conducting routine inspections. Dr. Kaur stood nearby, container in hand, confusion evident on her face as sweat beaded on her forehead.

The medical staff exchanged looks before one signaled to the dog handler, directing the overheated animal toward Dr. Kaur. I immediately recognized the unauthorized security check—the kind of practical joke that heat and boredom sometimes inspired among junior personnel.

I moved forward, raising my hand to stop the procedure before it could embarrass everyone involved.

The dog circled Dr. Kaur once, its tongue hanging out from the heat before the handler pulled it back. "Nothing detected, sir," the handler reported, more interested in getting his animal back to shade than in the inspection results.

Dr. Kaur's expression transformed from confusion to anger as she realized what had occurred—even in this heat, the indignity of being subjected to an impromptu security check by junior personnel was unacceptable. She set the container down and walked away stiffly, her professional dignity intact despite the circumstances.

I turned toward the medical staff, my gaze conveying more reprimand than words could express in the moment. They stepped back, recognizing their prank had crossed a line that shouldn't have been crossed, regardless of the stress everyone was under.

I inspected the container. Fruit custard, carefully prepared and kept cool with ice packs surrounding the inner container.

The next morning at the Alpha checkpoint, Dr. Kaur's vehicle approached through the heat shimmer. I stood at my usual position, but she drove through without the usual courtesy stop, eyes focused straight ahead. The deliberate avoidance was more cutting than any words could have been.

That evening, I inspected the camp perimeter alone, the heat finally beginning to ease as the sun set behind the mountains. The mobile phone in my side pocket buzzed once—my sister responding to my brief message about the day's complications.

Her reply was typically direct: "Fix it."

Dawn broke on the fifth day with no relief from the punishing heat. I completed my morning briefing with the joint security team, then made an unscheduled stop at the village sarpanch's residence. I emerged moments later with something concealed in my hand, a small gesture that I hoped might repair the damage caused by yesterday's incident.

When Dr. Kaur's vehicle approached the midday checkpoint, I stepped into the road despite the blazing sun, raising my hand in the standard stop signal.

"Security check?" she asked, her voice professional but distant, sweat glistening on her forehead despite the vehicle's air conditioning.

I circled to the driver's side and placed a single red rose on the steering wheel—a flower that had somehow maintained its beauty despite the oppressive heat. Then I stepped back and resumed my formal stance, signaling her to proceed.

Dr. Kaur stared at the rose, then at me. Her expression remained unchanged for several moments—a professional mask that revealed nothing. Then she shifted gears and drove forward without acknowledgment.

Fifty meters ahead, her brake lights illuminated. The vehicle reversed slowly, stopping beside me despite the heat that made standing on the asphalt feel like walking on coals. Without a word, she reached for the rose and scattered its petals toward me before driving away, leaving me standing in a shower of red fragments that seemed to burn brighter than the sun itself.

I stood motionless, red petals settling on my uniform like drops of blood, as the convoy continued under my protection. My radio operator caught my eye, awaiting instructions while wiping sweat from his equipment. I responded with the hand signal to maintain positions, my professional demeanor unbroken despite the heat and the personal drama unfolding.

But as I turned to scan the eastern ridgeline, something had fundamentally shifted in the security operation. The oppressive heat that had been merely a tactical challenge now carried the weight of personal stakes—I had something to protect beyond duty and protocol, something that made every decision more complex and every risk more personal.

The final two days of the Yatra stretched ahead, each hour bringing temperatures that tested human endurance while deepening the complicated dance between professional obligation and personal connection. In the shimmering heat haze that rose from the sacred grounds, the line between duty and desire had become as blurred as the horizon itself.

**August heat blessed the sacred way,*
Pilgrims walked where gods had trod.
Her medical tent saved souls each day
While I stood guard with faith in God.

Pink tiffin came like answered prayer,
Sweet kheer cooling bitter doubt.
In holy work, we formed a pair—
*Her healing, my protective route.**

❀❀❀

CHAPTER 13

"TRIAD OF CRISIS"

August 8, 2014–Day 5 of the Yatra.

The fifth day of the Buda Amarnath Yatra dawned with the sun already blazing like an angry eye. At 0830 hours, the temperature was climbing toward another punishing 36°C, and the temple complex pulsed with devotees whose endurance was being tested by both spiritual fervor and physical extremes.

I positioned myself at the command post, scanning the pilgrimage routes through air that shimmered like water. My men patrolled in established patterns, communicating through practiced hand signals while constantly seeking whatever shade was available. The heat made even thinking an effort, turning simple decisions into complex calculations of risk versus benefit.

The signal-jamming vehicle hummed twenty meters to my left, its cooling fans working overtime in a losing battle against the oppressive temperature. Havildar Mehta monitored the equipment with the grim determination of someone fighting both technology and climate.

"Sahab," Mehta's voice cut through the suffocating air, thick with concern. "Detector showing anomalous readings."

Four quick strides brought me to his position, the sweat immediately beading on my forehead despite the brief movement. The display showed rhythmic spikes—the unmistakable signature of a remote detonator. My stomach clenched like a fist closing around the ice.

"Location?" A one-word question, my voice barely audible above the humming equipment.

"Eastern sector. Parking area." Mehta adjusted the directional antenna with hands slick from perspiration, the device's beeping accelerating like a heart monitor during cardiac arrest.

Calculations ran automatically through my heat-fogged mind: eastern parking area, approximately two hundred vehicles baking in the sun, fifty-meter blast radius, three hundred civilians at risk. The heat made everything more dangerous—stressed people, failing equipment, shortened tempers. I keyed my radio.

"Alpha teams, silent alert. Possible IED, eastern parking. Normal patrol patterns. No visible reaction."

My men received the transmission without breaking strid. Only subtle shifts in posture betrayed their heightened alertness—hands closer to weapons that were too hot to touch, eyes straining against the blazing glare. Visible disruption could trigger a waiting bomber who might be watching from the shade.

"Signal strength increasing," Mehta reported, wiping sweat from his eyes with his sleeve. "Definite electronic signature."

Sweat poured down my face despite the morning hour, making my vision blur. I dispatched two plain-clothes soldiers with handheld detectors, using only a sharp nod and two brief hand signals. Temple ceremonies continued undisturbed, though I could see pilgrims already seeking shelter from the oppressive sun.

My radio vibrated against my sweat-soaked shirt. "Sahab," came Lance Naik Dhawan's whisper, his voice strained from the heat. "Signal isolated. Row three, fifth vehicle from the western end."

"Description?" I asked, my throat already dry as desert sand despite drinking water constantly.

"Red Maruti 800, sir. Dr. Kaur's car."

My blood turned to ice water despite the blazing heat around me. For a heartbeat, military training battled with personal feelings while the sun beat down mercilessly. Training won, but at a cost I could feel in my chest.

"Confirm. Initiate Protocol Kilo. Discreet evacuation. Vehicle owner's location?"

"Temple security log shows Dr. Kaur signed in ninety minutes ago. Currently at medical tent treating heat casualties."

Facts assembled with cold precision despite the oppressive conditions: Jasleen arrived early, parked her car in the blazing hot, and had been working in the medical tent treating pilgrims suffering from heat exhaustion. If she planted the device, she was safely away from the blast zone. If innocent, someone had used her vehicle while she was saving lives.

"Surveillance on the medical tent. No approach. EOD team to the parking area. Alpha Two, silent evacuation, eastern quadrant. Gas leak cover."

The bomb disposal team arrived in unmarked vehicles, their equipment cases designed to look like routine maintenance gear. Even in the punishing heat, they worked with methodical precision, though I could see sweat pouring from their faces as they approached the car.

Their handheld detector confirmed Mehta's reading—live explosive device, professionally constructed, hidden in the trunk where the metal would be scalding hot to touch.

"Lieutenant, positive confirmation. Military-grade components. Timer active. Heat may be affecting stability."

No crude terrorist device—this was sophisticated, indicating either foreign involvement or military expertise. In Jasleen's car. Under a sun that made every metal surface untouchable and every decision more desperate.

As EOD specialists worked in the punishing heat, their cooling vests already soaked through, my radio crackled with a second alert from Inspector Sharma, temple perimeter security.

"Bajrang Dal procession approaching from the north. Sixty participants, unauthorized route. Muslim residents gathering in response. Heat making everyone agitated. Confrontation imminent."

My jaw tightened like steel heated in a forge. Two security threats converging simultaneously in oppressive conditions that made everyone's judgment suspect—rarely a coincidence. The IED might be a diversion for sectarian violence, or vice versa, with the heat amplifying every tension.

"Hold position. Alpha Three team deploying. Keep procession minimum two hundred meters from the complex."

A single hand signal to my second-in-command mobilized the team despite the energy-sapping conditions. The eastern evacuation continued under the gas leak pretext while the bomb disposal team worked methodically in heat that threatened both their equipment and their endurance.

Now the difficult decision: approaching Dr. Kaur. Protocol demanded detention. Instinct screamed she was being framed. But the heat was affecting my judgment, making emotions run hotter and thoughts less clear.

I chose a path between duty and conviction.

"Medical tent status?" I radioed surveillance.

"Dr. Kaur treating patients. Five pilgrims with heat exhaustion waiting. Three assistants present. No suspicious behavior. Focused on medical emergencies."

I moved toward the medical area, every step on the blazing ground feeling like walking across coals. Through the tent opening, Jasleen checked an elderly woman's blood pressure while a fan barely stirred the stifling air. Calm, professional—no signs of the nervous tension typical of someone who had planted a bomb.

My radio vibrated urgently against my soaked shirt. "Police units approaching medical tent, tactical formation."

Before I could reach her, four police officers entered the tent, weapons visible, their uniforms dark with perspiration. The senior officer approached Jasleen directly while she knelt beside a heat stroke victim.

"Dr. Jasleen Kaur, you are under arrest for terrorist activities and endangering public safety."

The blood drained from her face, leaving her pale despite the oppressive heat. She froze, stethoscope still in hand, sweat beading on her forehead from stress rather than temperature. "What? There must be some mistake—"

"An explosive device has been located in your vehicle," the officer continued as his men moved forward with handcuffs that gleamed hot in the blazing light.

I stepped between them, my uniform already soaked through with sweat and stress. "Inspector, I'm the security officer. This falls under my jurisdiction."

His eyes narrowed, sweat streaming down his face. "With respect, Lieutenant, we have orders from the Intelligence Branch. We've been tracking her suspicious activities for weeks."

"I'm aware of the IED. My team discovered it."

"Then you're aware this woman has been under surveillance. Multiple suspicious communications, connections to sympathizers across the border."

Jasleen gasped behind me, the sound barely audible above the whirring of inadequate fans. "That's not true! I have family in Pakistan—cousins separated during Partition. Our communication is personal!"

"Lieutenant, step aside. This is a police matter now."

I remained motionless, aware of the line between duty and conviction blurring in the oppressive heat. Around us, patients waited for medical attention while their doctors faced arrest. "Inspector, Dr. Kaur has been working since early morning treating heat casualties. The device shows signs of recent installation—"

"She had accomplices or planted it before reporting for duty. Lieutenant, I won't ask again."

My radio crackled, breaking the standoff. "Bajrang Dal procession broke containment. Approaching temple perimeter. Crowd control needed immediately." The heat was making the volatile situation even more dangerous.

Military discipline reasserted itself despite the sweat pouring down my face. Two active threats required immediate attention, and the oppressive conditions were making everyone's judgment suspect. Personal feelings could not override thousands of pilgrims' safety, especially when heat exhaustion was already claiming victims.

"Secure the suspect," I told the police, stepping aside despite every instinct screaming against it. "Full procedural compliance expected."

The devastation on Jasleen's face cut through me like shrapnel heated white-hot. Her eyes—those eyes that had shown both fear and affection—now reflected pure betrayal that seemed to burn hotter than the sun above us.

"Murari," she whispered as they handcuffed her, my name barely audible in the stifling air. "You know me. You know I wouldn't—"

"Get her to the station," the inspector ordered, sweat dripping from his face onto his clipboard.

As they led her away, she looked back through the shimmering heat waves. "I trusted you," she said, voice breaking like glass in a furnace. "After everything, I finally trusted you."

The words struck deeper than any physical blow, made worse by the oppressive heat that seemed to amplify every emotion. I stood motionless, face masking my turmoil.

"We still have the Bajrang Dal situation. Heat's making everyone more aggressive. Possibly coordinated action—IED as a distraction, or vice versa."

I compartmentalized, pushing aside Jasleen's image while sweat stung my eyes. "Three teams, northern perimeter. Non-lethal equipment. Buffer zone between groups."

The procession appeared through the heat haze—saffron headbands, provocative chants, faces red from sun and anger. Opposing them, local Muslims gathered defensively, everyone more volatile. Between stood my men, discipline against sectarian tension.

I moved directly between the groups, signaling both for silence with my hands.

Their leader stepped forward, his face streaming with sweat. "A terrorist was just arrested—a Muslim woman planning to bomb pilgrims! In this heat, we won't tolerate".

I raised my hand sharply. "Security operations ongoing. Spreading unverified information endangers all present. Disperse or I shoot to kill you."

Major Isaac appeared silently beside me, his uniform as soaked as everyone else's. "Bomb neutralized. Sophisticated construction. Heat nearly triggered premature detonation.".

I nodded mechanically, watching as the Bajrang Dal members reluctantly withdrew to seek shade.

Back at the command post, I reassessed operations: bomb neutralized, suspect detained, confrontation averted. Tactical success was achieved despite conditions that tested everyone's limits.

Yet as I marked patrol patterns on maps, doubt surfaced—unprecedented in my career. What if Jasleen was innocent? What if she had been framed while dedicating herself to saving lives in impossible conditions?

The signal detector lay silent, its mission complete, but cooling fans still whirred desperately against the heat. Questions remained, pulsing like the blazing sun overhead—counting down to when I must choose between my uniform and my heart, while the temperature made every decision feel like walking through fire.

For the first time since commissioning, I questioned not my training, but the intelligence itself. In counterterrorism, doubt was a luxury none could afford— even certainty became suspect.

**The detector screamed through blazing air,*
Her car held death's metallic heart.
"Step aside!" they came for her,
My duty tore our love apart.

She whispered "Murari" like a prayer
While handcuffs caught the morning light.
I chose my oath, she chose despair—
The moment when our love took flight. *

CHAPTER 14

"WALK INTO WALNUT GROVE"

August 16, 2014

The Poonch District Court smelled of old wood and stale cigarettes. I sat in the witness box. "Lieutenant Murari Kumar," the judge's voice cut through the stuffy air, "you were present during the incident at Buda Amarnath temple?"

"Yes, Your Honor." My voice echoed in the nearly empty courtroom.

The Police Superintendent shifted in his chair, his belly straining against his khaki shirt. Sweat beads formed on his forehead as he'd been arguing for two hours why Dr. Jasleen Kaur should remain in custody—suspected terrorist activities, public safety concerns, flight risk.

"In your professional opinion as the security officer," the judge continued, adjusting wire-rimmed spectacles that kept sliding down his sweating nose, "did Dr. Kaur demonstrate any suspicious behavior during the Yatra?"

I paused, my mind racing through tactical calculations while sweat trickled down my back. Truth versus loyalty. Duty versus growing doubt. The courtroom fell silent except for the tick of the wall clock and the squeak of struggling ceiling fans.

"Your Honor, Dr. Kaur provided exemplary medical service throughout the pilgrimage. She treated over fifty heat exhaustion cases, worked fourteen-hour shifts in brutal conditions, and showed dedication to saving lives regardless of the patient's background."

The Police Superintendent's jaw tightened like a coiled spring. His pen snapped between his fingers, plastic cracking in the oppressive heat. "The IED found in her vehicle—" he began.

"Could have been planted by anyone with access to the parking area," I interrupted, my voice steady despite the sweat streaming down my face. "The device showed signs of a recent installation. Dr. Kaur had been in the medical tent for ninety minutes treating heat casualties before discovery."

The judge scribbled notes, his pen scratching across the yellow paper that was already curling from humidity. Twenty minutes later, he granted bail with conditions: no travel beyond district limits, weekly reporting to the police station, and surrender of passport.

As people filed out, their clothes sticking to their bodies from the oppressive humidity, the judge caught my eye. A subtle nod toward his chambers.

District Judge Ramesh Chandra's private office felt like stepping into another era. Law books lined the walls from floor to ceiling, their leather spines cracked with age. The smell of old paper mixed with sandalwood incense from a small shrine in the corner. He poured tea from a brass kettle, the liquid steaming in bone china cups that had seen better decades.

"Sit, Lieutenant." His voice carried the weight of thirty years on the bench. "Off the record."

I remained standing until he gestured more firmly, my uniform clinging uncomfortably to my skin.

"You know this region better than most outsiders," he began, stirring sugar into his tea with deliberate slowness. "But you're still an outsider."

The tea cup rattled against its saucer as I lifted it, betraying nerves amplified by the oppressive conditions.

"These mountain valleys have seen more betrayals than monsoons," Judge Chandra continued. "Beauty here often masks danger. A woman's smile can hide more secrets than a terrorist's bunker."

His eyes studied me over his tea cup while sweat beaded on both our foreheads. "You testified with conviction today. But conviction can be a weakness when dealing with matters of the heart."

My collar felt like a noose in the humid air. "Sir, I simply provided factual observations—"

"Lieutenant." His voice cut sharp as a courtroom gavel. "I've seen good men destroyed by beautiful women with divided loyalties. In Kashmir, family ties cross borders like morning mist. What seems like love might be carefully crafted recruitment."

The sandalwood incense made my nose itch, or maybe it was the growing anxiety crawling up my spine like monsoon humidity.

"A honey trap doesn't always involve blackmail," he continued. "Sometimes it's just genuine affection mixed with strategic information gathering. The most dangerous spies believe in their own innocence."

He set down his cup with a soft clink that seemed loud in the stifling air. "Watch yourself, son. Your testimony today saved her freedom. Make sure her freedom doesn't cost you your honor."

I walked out of the courthouse feeling like I'd been stripped of my rank and dressed in civilian doubt. The afternoon sun beat down on the courthouse steps, making the concrete too hot to touch. Street vendors called out their wares—fresh corn roasted over coal fires, the smoke mixing with diesel fumes from passing trucks.

Dr. Jasleen walked beside me down the courthouse steps, her dupatta draped over her head like armor against staring eyes. Dark circles under her eyes spoke of sleepless nights in custody, but even exhausted, she carried herself with a quiet dignity that made my chest tighten.

"Thank you," she said simply as we reached the street where the asphalt was soft from the heat. "For speaking the truth."

"I spoke what I observed," I replied, my voice more formal than intended while sweat ran down my back.

As we approached the courthouse gate where lawyers and relatives waited in whatever shade they could find, she suddenly stopped. "Lieutenant, may I borrow your pen for a moment?"

I handed her my service pen. Her fingers brushed mine as she took it, the contact sending electricity up my arm despite the oppressive conditions. She quickly wrote something on a scrap of paper from her purse, then handed both back.

The paper read: "ALG gate, 6 PM. If you want to understand." The ink was already smearing slightly from humidity.

Before I could respond, she had disappeared into the crowd, leaving me standing there with the weight of decision pressing down like the monsoon air itself.

The Advanced Landing Ground gate stood like a sentinel at the edge of military territory. I arrived at 1800 hours sharp, my civilian clothes—jeans and a simple shirt—feeling strange after months of uniform precision. My service pistol remained hidden beneath the shirt.

Her red Maruti 800 idled near the checkpoint, exhaust fumes mixing with the evening air that carried scents of approaching rain and distant wood smoke. Through the windshield, I could see her profile, sharp cheekbones catching the diffused light through storm clouds, hair pulled back in a simple ponytail that made her look younger despite the ordeal she'd endured.

When I approached, she leaned over and opened the passenger door. "Get in."

The interior smelled like vanilla and medical antiseptic—a combination that somehow made perfect sense for her. The seat felt warm where her body heat had touched the fabric. My knees brushed against the dashboard as I folded myself into the compact space, suddenly aware of how small the car was, how close we'd be.

"Where are we going?" I asked as she shifted into gear.

"Somewhere we can talk without walls having ears," she replied, her voice carrying an edge I hadn't heard before.

She drove through Poonch town, past the bazaar where vendors were closing their stalls against the approaching storm, past the mosque where evening prayers had just concluded, past the last checkpoint where a bored-looking constable waved us through without inspection.

The road began climbing into the hills, winding through villages that grew smaller and more scattered with each kilometer. My training kicked in automatically, memorizing routes, calculating distances, and noting terrain features. But I found myself distracted by the way her hands gripped the steering wheel, the way she kept glancing in the rearview mirror as if checking for followers.

"Nervous?" I asked.

"Aren't you?" she replied without taking her eyes off the road.

We passed the last proper village—a cluster of stone houses with tin roofs, smoke rising from evening cooking fires, children playing cricket in the fading light before the storm hit. Beyond that, the settlements became sparse: isolated farmhouses, shepherd huts, patches of terraced fields carved into impossible slopes.

The monsoon clouds were building into towering thunderheads, promising relief from the day's heat. In the distance, I could see the silver line that marked the LoC fence, that ribbon of wire and concrete that divided not just countries but families, dreams, and destinies.

"How much farther?" I asked, my voice tighter than intended.

"Just beyond the last house," she said softly.

My mouth went dry. Beyond the last house meant the dangerous zone between civilian settlements and the LoC fence—where only soldiers and smugglers dared to go, where Pakistani snipers could take clean shots, where ambushes waited in the gathering storm clouds.

Every survival instinct screamed at me to tell her to stop, to turn around, to get back to safe territory. But something in her voice—a vulnerability that sounded like truth—kept me silent.

We drove past a single farmhouse, its windows glowing yellow against the darkening sky. An old man sat on the front porch, smoking a hookah, his weathered face turning to watch our car pass. Beyond that, the road became little more than a dirt track.

"Here," she said, pulling off beside a grove of walnut trees.

The silence after she cut the engine felt profound despite the rumbling thunder in the distance. No traffic, no human voices, just the whisper of wind through leaves and the distant sound of water running over stones. The air that came through the open windows carried the green smell of growing things and something else—the metallic taste of an approaching storm that every soldier learns to recognize.

She stepped out of the car, her dupatta fluttering in the pre-storm breeze like a prayer flag. Her hair, freed from its usual professional constraints, caught the last dying light and threw it back in waves of gold and copper. She wore a simple salwar kameez the color of new leaves, making her seem to blend with the landscape around us.

"Come," she said, her voice barely above a whisper.

I followed her through the grove, my feet crunching on fallen walnuts, the sound unnaturally loud in the stillness broken only by distant thunder. Every shadow could hide a sniper. Every rustle of leaves could mask approaching hostiles. My hand instinctively moved toward my concealed weapon.

But she walked with the confidence of someone who belonged here, stepping carefully over roots and stones until we emerged into a small clearing on the hillside.

"This is my favorite place in the world," she said, settling onto a flat boulder that jutted from the hillside like nature's own observation platform.

The view spread before us like a tactical map come to life. The valley dropped away in terraced steps, each level marked by stone walls built by hands long dead. Villages dotted the landscape like scattered coins, their lights beginning to twinkle as darkness approached with the storm. And beyond it all, snaking across the hills like a scar, the LoC fence gleamed dull silver against the storm clouds.

"When I was small," she continued, her voice carrying that musical quality that made every word sound like poetry, "my mother would bring me here to pick walnuts. She'd tell me stories about her childhood, about the time before the fence existed."

I sat beside her, close enough to smell the vanilla scent that seemed to be her natural fragrance, far enough to maintain tactical awareness while storm clouds gathered overhead. The stone felt cool through my jeans, solid and real in a world that suddenly seemed filled with questions.

"The view from here," she said, standing and moving to the edge of the clearing, "shows you how meaningless lines on maps really are."

I joined her, and the valley spread below us like God's own painting. Villages on both sides of the invisible border, their lights beginning to twinkle despite the approaching storm. Streams that flowed regardless of nationality. Birds that flew where they pleased without showing passports.

And then I saw it.

In the far distance, barely visible through the evening haze, a small green flag fluttered from what looked like an innocent cluster of rocks. But my trained eye caught the telltale signs, too-straight lines in the natural landscape, metallic glints where metal shouldn't be, and the unnatural absence of vegetation in a perfect firing arc.

Pakistani observation post. Concealed bunker. Active enemy position with a clear line of sight to our location.

My blood turned to ice water. We were in their crosshairs. Had been since we arrived. Every tactical alarm in my brain started screaming to withdraw or to move to safety, or take cover.

The first drops of rain began to fall, bringing blessed relief from the day's heat. The air suddenly smelled clean and fresh.

"Murari," she said, turning toward me as the gentle rain began to fall, and my name on her lips sounded like prayer and confession combined. "I need you to know something."

Lightning flickered in the distance, and thunder rumbled closer now. This was it—the moment of truth.

"The night they arrested me," she continued, rain drops glistening on her face, "I thought my life was over. Not because of prison, but because I thought you believed I was guilty."

She stepped closer, eliminating the last space between us. I could feel the warmth radiating from her body, hear the whisper of her breathing, see my own reflection in her eyes.

"When you testified for me today, when you told the truth despite everything..." Her voice caught like fabric on thorns. "I realized something I'd been trying to deny."

The rain was falling steadily now, bringing blessed relief from the heat.

"I've fallen in love with you," she whispered.

The words hit me like lightning—unexpected, devastating, changing everything in an instant. My breath caught in my throat. My training screamed warnings while my heart shouted triumph.

"I know the complications," she continued, her free hand coming up to touch my face, fingertips tracing the line of my jaw. "I know the dangers. I know your duty comes first. But I couldn't pretend anymore."

Her touch felt like electricity, like fire, like coming home after a long war. I leaned into it despite every protocol I'd ever learned.

"In this work," she whispered, her breath warm against my ear, "I see so much pain, so much fear. People come to me bleeding from wounds that politics created, divided by suspicions that fear planted. But when I'm with you, I remember that healing is still possible."

"Jasleen..." I began, but she moved closer, her body pressing against mine.

"Don't think," she whispered, her breath warm against my ear. "For once in your military life, just feel."

Time suspended like the rain clouds overhead. The war, the suspicions, the investigations—all of it faded until there was only this moment, this woman, this connection that defied every protocol I'd ever learned.

I kissed her.

Her lips tasted like rain and secrets and the salt of tears I hadn't seen her shed. Soft and warm and utterly perfect. She melted against me, her hands finding the back of my neck, fingers tangling in my hair while the cooling rain washed away the day's oppression.

Somewhere in the distance, thunder rolled across the valley, the same sound that echoed in the hills where men fought and died for invisible lines. The storm seemed to bridge the gap between worlds, between hearts that had been divided by politics but united by something stronger than borders or suspicion.

When we finally broke apart, both breathing hard, the rain had brought blessed coolness to the air.

"What happens now?" she asked, her forehead resting against mine while rain ran down our faces.

I looked into her eyes, searching one last time for deception, for calculation, for anything that might confirm the judge's warnings. All I saw was vulnerability and hope and a love that mirrored my own, cleansed by the rain like everything else in this moment.

In the distance, lights twinkled on both sides of the invisible border, while rain fell equally on all of them, indifferent to the lines drawn on maps by men who had never stood in this place, never felt what we felt.

"I don't know," I admitted. "But we'll figure it out."

She smiled then—the first genuine, unguarded smile I'd ever seen from her, made more beautiful by the rain that cooled her flushed cheeks. It transformed her face completely, erasing the lines of worry and fear, making her look like the girl who used to come here with her mother to pick walnuts and dream of a world without violence.

As we walked back to her car through the refreshing rain, I realized the most dangerous mission of my life had just begun. Not the kind fought with weapons and tactics, but the kind that required courage of an entirely different sort.

The kind that required trusting your heart in a world determined to break it, while the cooling rain promised that even the most oppressive heat eventually breaks, and something beautiful can grow in the aftermath.

**She drove toward the walnut trees*
Where monsoon clouds gathered their might.
"My family," she said with plea,
"Lives beyond the fence's sight."

Rain washed clean the burning doubt
As lips found lips in storm's embrace.
Truth flowing in, fear flowing out—
*Love blooming in that sacred space.**

❦ ❦ ❦

CHAPTER 15

"MENDHAR DEPLOYMENT"

August 20, 2014

The morning call came at 0530 hours. My radio crackled to life just as I was lacing my boots, still thinking about five nights ago—Jasleen's hand in mine, the way starlight had caught in her hair, the taste of rain on her lips.

"Lieutenant Murari, report to Major Isaac's office. Immediate."

My stomach dropped like a stone falling into deep water. I'd been expecting this call, dreading it, knowing that our stolen moments couldn't stay hidden forever in a place where everything was watched, measured, reported.

The walk to Major Isaac's office felt like approaching an enemy bunker. My palms started sweating—not from the morning air, but from walking into an ambush I couldn't avoid.

Major Isaac sat behind his metal desk like a judge preparing for execution. Intelligence files spread before him like evidence at a court martial. His coffee mug steamed in the cool air.

"Sit down, Murari." His voice carried disappointment mixed with professional duty.

I lowered myself into the chair across from him.

He opened the first file without looking at me. "Seventeen phone calls in the past two weeks." His finger traced down a list. "Daily vehicle movement patterns showing deviation from assigned routes. Satellite imagery of unauthorized stops at civilian locations."

"As your friend," he continued, finally meeting my eyes, "I'm asking you to step back from this path. As your intelligence officer, I'm telling you it leads to court martial and disgrace."

"Sir," I began, but he held up a hand.

"Money transfers through hawala networks."

My vision blurred. "Those could be family members, sir. Partition separated many—

"Or they could be handlers." His voice cut through my explanation. "Intelligence is about patterns, Lieutenant. And the pattern here screams recruitment, manipulation, honey trap."

The word 'honey trap' echoed in my brain. Could everything between Jasleen and me be a carefully constructed lie? The thought made my stomach twist like a knife being turned.

"You're compromised, son." Major Isaac's voice softened. "Whether she's innocent or guilty, your objectivity is gone. That makes you dangerous to yourself and your unit."

I stared at my hands, noting how they trembled. The calluses from weapon handling stood out against my palm lines—physical proof of my military identity, now under threat.

"What are you recommending, sir?"

He closed the files with finality. "Forward deployment to Mendhar sector for artillery observation duties. Immediate assignment. You'll establish surveillance of the Balakote area, one kilometer ahead of the LoC fence. Your task—direct artillery and mortar fire on enemy positions, locate and destroy their gun positions."

The blood drained from my face. Mendhar was the most dangerous assignment in the sector—where officers went to prove themselves or die trying. Pakistani snipers had clear shots during daylight hours. Mortar attacks came daily.

"This is front-line combat duty," I said quietly.

"This is where we need our best artillery observer." His eyes hardened. "A soldier of the Indian Army. Not some lovesick boy who forgot his oath."

The insult stung. Heat flushed up my neck. But beneath the anger, I knew he was right. Somewhere between stolen kisses and midnight conversations, I had lost sight of my primary duty.

"When do I deploy, sir?"

"0800 hours. This is a sixty-day minimum deployment. You'll have sophisticated surveillance equipment—thermal imaging, range finders, night vision systems." He stood. "Your primary mission is to observe Balakote area and coordinate counter-battery fire. Secondary task—eliminate their mortar and artillery positions through precision targeting."

I saluted and turned to leave.

"And Murari? No communication with civilian personnel during deployment. All radio traffic will be monitored for operational security."

"I hope you find what you're looking for up there, son. Whether it's clarity or redemption through service."

I had forty-five minutes to gather my gear and say goodbye to the woman who had turned my ordered world upside down. My hands shook as I stuffed equipment into my rucksack—spare ammunition, field rations, water purification tablets, and extra batteries for radio equipment.

The walk to the hospital felt like approaching my own execution. Morning mist clung to the valley floor. The smell of wood smoke from village cooking fires mixed with eucalyptus trees.

I found Jasleen in the emergency ward, her dupatta had slipped back, revealing the curve of her neck where I'd kissed her just days before.

"Jasleen." My voice came out rougher than intended.

She looked up, and I watched her face transform as she read the bad news in my expression. Her eyes filled with fear.

"What's wrong?" she whispered, abandoning her patient to step closer.

"I'm being deployed to Mendhar sector. Artillery observation mission. Deploying in thirty minutes."

The color drained from her face. She reached out as if to touch me, then remembered where we were and pulled her hand back.

"That's the most dangerous sector," she whispered. "The forward positions where they send—"

"Where they send their best artillery officers," I completed, trying to sound confident.

"For how long?" Her voice was barely audible above the hospital noise.

"Sixty days minimum." I couldn't tell her that artillery observers at Mendhar had the highest casualty rate in the sector. Couldn't say that Major Isaac expected me to either come back a proven soldier or not come back at all.

"Is this because of us?" she asked.

I nodded. Around us, the hospital continued its routine—medical emergencies, the constant battle against suffering. But in our small bubble of heartbreak, none of that seemed to matter.

"I'm sorry," she whispered. "I should have known this would happen. Should have been stronger, should have kept my distance."

"Don't." The word came out sharper than I intended. "Don't apologize for being the best thing that's happened to me in this godforsaken place."

She smiled then, but it was the saddest expression I'd ever seen.

"Will you be able to call?"

"Radio protocols will be monitored." I couldn't tell her that any attempt to contact her would be seen as confirmation of compromise, grounds for court martial.

We stood there for a moment while our hearts were breaking. The distance between us—just three feet of hospital linoleum—felt wider than the Poonch valley itself.

"Be safe," she said finally.

"Always am." The lie tasted bitter.

I turned to leave, but her voice stopped me.

"Murari?"

I looked back.

"When you come down from the mountain," she said quietly, "I'll be here."

The promise hit me hard. Because we both knew that men who went to Mendhar observation post didn't always come back down. And even if they did, they were usually different people—changed by what they'd seen, hardened by what they'd survived.

The helicopter carried me and crates of sophisticated surveillance equipment to Mendhar sector. Twenty-five minutes through thin mountain air, flying over terrain that grew increasingly hostile—dusky peaks, wide valleys, the silver line of the LoC fence marking the edge of Indian territory.

The forward observation base sat on a rocky outcrop overlooking Balakote area. Not a permanent posting, but a tactical position equipped with state-of-the-art surveillance technology. Bunkers built into the hillside, reinforced observation posts, communication equipment that could direct artillery fire with pinpoint accuracy.

Captain Sahil Sharma met me at the landing zone, his face weathered by months of front-line duty. He looked like someone who'd seen too much combat in too little time.

"Welcome to the front line," he said, his voice carrying the weight of experience. "Pakistani positions are clearly visible from here. Their mortar teams fire at us daily between 0800 and 1600 hours. Artillery duels every evening around sunset."

He led me to the main observation post, equipped with thermal imaging scopes, laser range finders, and night vision systems. "Your job is to spot their gun positions and call-in counter-battery fire. See that ridge at two o'clock? They have at least three 120mm mortar tubes there. They've been pounding our positions for weeks."

Through the high-powered scope, I could see the enemy positions clearly—camouflaged firing positions, ammunition bunkers, the telltale signs of artillery emplacements. This wasn't just observation—this was direct combat against enemy gunners who were trying to kill us every day.

"Rules of engagement?" I asked.

"Locate, identify, and destroy. You have the authority to call fire missions on confirmed enemy positions." Sharma adjusted the scope. "Lieutenant, up here you're not just watching—you're fighting a daily artillery war."

The handover briefing covered sophisticated equipment operation, fire control procedures, and communication protocols with our own artillery units positioned kilometers behind us. This was precision warfare—using technology and tactics to eliminate enemy threats before they could eliminate us.

As Sharma's helicopter disappeared into the valley below, I realized this wasn't punishment duty. This was where the

Indian Army sent officers they trusted with million-dollar equipment and life-or-death targeting decisions. The isolation felt different now—not exile, but responsibility.

My radio crackled at 1100 hours. "Mendhar OP, this is Thunder Base. Radio check, over."

"Thunder Base, Mendhar OP. Signal strength five, over."

"Copy, Mendhar. Maintain surveillance on Balakote sector. Intelligence reports increased enemy artillery activity in your area."

"Understood, Thunder Base. Thermal imaging shows movement near enemy mortar positions. Standing by for fire mission."

"Roger, Mendhar. You are cleared to engage confirmed targets. Thunder Base out."

I settled into the observation routine—continuous surveillance through thermal scopes, recording enemy movement patterns, calculating firing coordinates for counter-battery missions. The sophisticated equipment required total concentration, but it also gave me the power to strike back at enemies who had been attacking our positions with impunity.

During brief quiet moments—when the enemy positions seemed inactive and the valley lay still under afternoon sun—my mind would drift back to her. The way she'd said my name like a prayer. The way her dupatta had fluttered in the evening breeze. The way she'd promised to wait.

**"Report to Mendhar," Isaac said,*
"Where warriors go to prove their worth."
The deadliest post filled me with dread—
My love just found, now torn from earth.

Her eyes held tears she couldn't hide
As morning light blessed her sweet face.
"I'll wait," she whispered by my side,
*"Until you return to this place."**

CHAPTER 16

"WHEN HEARTS TURN TO STONE"

September 15, 2014–Day 26 at Mendhar

Day fourteen at Mendhar observation post. The morning alarm wasn't my watch—it was the familiar whistle of incoming 120mm mortar rounds. My body rolled off the cot and hit the concrete floor before my brain fully woke up. Muscle memory. Pure survival instinct.

Thump-thump-thump.

Three rounds landed fifty meters from our position. Close enough that dust rained from the bunker ceiling like snow. Close enough that the concussion made my ribs vibrate like guitar strings. My ears rang with that high-pitched whine that follows every near miss—a sound that now played constantly in my head, even during quiet moments.

"Morning prayer call from Pakistan," muttered Havildar Ravi, spitting dust from his mouth. His joke fell flat. Everything felt flat now.

I reached for my binoculars with hands that no longer shook. That worried me more than the trembling used to. Fear keeps you alive. When you stop feeling afraid, you start making mistakes.

Through the scope, I spotted the telltale smoke rising from their mortar position. Grid reference Papa Kilo 247-891. Same position they'd used yesterday. Same position they'd use tomorrow. Everything had become predictable, mechanical, routine.

"Fire mission," I spoke into the magneto phone, cranking the handle with practiced efficiency. "Grid Papa Kilo 247-891. Enemy mortar position. Three tubes observed firing."

"Fire mission, grid Papa Kilo 247-891, out."

Thirty-seven seconds later, our own mortars screamed overhead. I watched through the scope as our shells impacted exactly where I'd called them. Dirt and smoke erupted from their position. Probably killed two or three Pakistani soldiers having their morning tea.

I felt nothing. No satisfaction, no regret, no human emotion at all. Just the mechanical calculation—threat eliminated, mission successful, next target.

This was what they meant by battle fatigue. When killing becomes as routine as brushing your teeth.

Day 28. The taste of cordite hung in the air like morning mist. My uniform reeked of sweat, gun oil, and the metallic smell of explosives. When I tried to remember what vanilla smelled like—Jasleen's hair, her dupatta, that sweet scent that used to make my chest tighten with longing.

Now when I closed my eyes and tried to summon that memory, all I could smell was smoke and death.

The magneto phone buzzed. I cranked the handle, lifting the heavy handset to my ear.

"Mendhar OP, Thunder Base. Mule supply drop incoming. ETA thirty-five minutes."

"Copy, Thunder Base."

Forty minutes later, the mule train arrived with supplies. Among the ammunition boxes and medical supplies, Naik Pathaniya handed me something that made my breath catch.

A pink tiffin box.

The same bright pink that had seemed so alien in our world of olive drab and camouflage. My hands trembled as I took it—the first emotion I'd felt in weeks.

"Madam ne bheja hai, sir," Pathaniya said softly.

Dr. Jasleen had sent food. Again. Even knowing I was deployed to the most dangerous sector, even with radio silence maintained for operational security, she'd found a way to care for me.

I opened the container with fingers that suddenly remembered how to feel. Nihari gosht. Real, honest-to-God home-cooked mutton nihari. The smell hit me like a physical force—turmeric and coriander, garam masala and fresh cilantro. And underneath it all, the faintest hint of vanilla from her hands that had prepared it.

For a moment, the concrete bunker faded away. I was back in that walnut grove, rain falling on our faces, her lips tasting like secrets and promises. The memory tasted like hope and possibility and everything this godforsaken mountain had burned out of me.

Then a mortar round exploded sixty meters away, and I was back in hell.

I ate the gosht slowly, but it had gone cold during the long journey. The taste was strange on my tongue—still delicious, but somehow different when eaten in a bunker that reeked of cordite and fear. My mind calculated the logistics: how had she managed this delivery? My heart warmed at the simple kindness, while battlefield intuition screamed warnings about security breaches and inappropriate contact.

Day 35. The magneto phone had become my lifeline to the world beyond killing. Major Ashish's voice crackled through the static.

"How are you holding up, Murari?"

"Operational, sir." The standard response. The safe response.

"That's not what I asked." His voice carried the concern of someone who'd been where I was, who understood the weight pressing down on my shoulders. "How is your health? Do you need anything from the base?"

"I'm managing, sir."

"Lieutenant, you've been up there five weeks. Even our best officers rotate out after thirty days in that sector."

Through the observation port, I watched Pakistani positions through thermal scopes. Green shapes moving like ghosts across my field of view. Potential targets. Possible threats. Never human beings with families and fears and dreams of home.

"The mission requires continuity, sir. I know their patterns now. Their timing, their positions, their weaknesses."

"Murari." Major Ashish's voice grew gentle, paternal. "You have people down here worried about you. Not just your military family—the doctor who keeps sending food. We need you alive and sane, not just operational."

The doctor. Jasleen. Her name still hit me like shrapnel, sudden and sharp. I'd been protecting myself from thinking about her, building walls around memories that could compromise my tactical focus.

"I understand, sir."

"Do you? Because ignoring your own welfare isn't heroism, Lieutenant. It's stupidity."

"Sir, human intelligence reports suspicious movement in Sector Charlie. Local source says three armed men crossed the fence last night."

I nodded, studying the map. Red pins marked enemy positions. Blue pins marked our own. Green pins marked suspected infiltration routes. The map looked like a violent constellation, every star representing potential death.

"Deploy observation team to Point Tango," I ordered, pointing to the high ridge. "Maintain visual contact. Rules of engagement—shoot when targets confirmed."

My words came out like machine gun bullets—short, precise, emotionless. The man who had once worried about pointing guns at a woman getting water now ordered soldiers to kill strangers without hesitation.

At 1430 hours, the crack of rifle fire echoed from Point Tango. Through my scope, I watched muzzle flashes wink in the distant trees. Our boys were in contact.

The radio crackled. "Contact, contact, contact. Three enemy personnel engaged. One down, two withdrawing toward fence."

"Roger," I replied, already adjusting coordinates for artillery support. "Fire mission follows."

Two minutes later, our shells turned the infiltration route into a crater. Another routine engagement, another tactical success, another few lives extinguished like candle flames.

The silence afterward felt heavier than the explosions. In that quiet, my mind tried to drift back to softer things—a woman's laugh, the taste of gajar ka halwa, the warmth of fingers intertwined with mine. But those memories felt like someone else's life, viewed through thick glass, too distant to touch.

Day 42. Lance Naik Suresh found me at 0300 hours, hunched over firing charts with calculations sprawled across three notebooks. The mathematics of murder had become my only companion.

"Sir, Major Isaac sahib wants to speak with you."

The magneto phone crackled as I cranked the handle. Major Isaac's voice came through clear and concerned.

"Murari, I've been reviewing your fire mission reports. Forty-three confirmed enemy casualties in six weeks. That's exceptional tactical performance."

"Thank you, sir."

"It's also inhuman. No officer should carry that kind of killing load alone." His pause stretched through the static. "I'm recommending immediate rotation for medical evaluation."

"Sir, the sector requires..." the line went dead.

Day 47. Dawn broke with the usual symphony of violence. Pakistani mortars had been pounding our positions since 0530 hours, their rounds walking closer to our bunker with each salvo. I crouched at the observation post, adjusting coordinates for counter-battery fire.

"Fire mission" I spoke into the magneto phone. "Grid Papa Kilo 389-647. Enemy mortar section, three tubes confirmed. Immediate suppression required."

"Shot out."

I pressed my eye to the spotter scope, watching for our shells to impact. The first salvo landed fifty meters short.

"Add fifty, fire for effect."

The second salvo was perfect—four high-explosive rounds landing directly on target. Through the scope, I watched the enemy position disappear in smoke and flame. Another tactical success. Another few lives were extinguished.

I was reaching for my logbook when something hot and sharp slammed into my left shoulder, spinning me around and dropping me to the concrete floor.

The world exploded in pain and confusion. Blood soaked through my uniform, spreading like spilled tea. A piece of shrapnel from a near miss, probably no bigger than a coin, but it felt like being struck by lightning.

"Sir! Medic!" Havildar Ravi's voice seemed to come from underwater.

Hands pressed against my shoulder, applying pressure to stop the bleeding. The pain was extraordinary—the first purely physical sensation I'd felt in weeks that wasn't dulled by emotional numbness.

"It's not deep," the medic announced after cutting away my shirt. "But you need proper medical attention. This is evacuation-worthy."

"No," I tried to protest, but my voice came out weak. "Mission continuity requires..."

"Mission continuity requires live officers, not dead heroes," Major Ashish's voice crackled through the radio. "Evac helicopter inbound. That's an order, Lieutenant."

As they loaded me onto the stretcher, I caught sight of my reflection in a broken piece of mirror embedded in the bunker wall. The man staring back had my face but different eyes. Eyes that had seen too much. Eyes that had forgotten how to see beauty, only threats and targets and tactical advantages.

The helicopter ride to Jammu Military Hospital passed in a haze of pain medication and exhaustion. Forty-seven days of accumulated fatigue hit me all at once, my body finally allowing itself to feel the weight of constant vigilance.

In the clean white hospital room, with nurses checking my vitals and doctors examining my wound, I felt like an alien visitor from a world of concrete and violence. The antiseptic smell reminded me of something—vanilla? No, that was memory playing tricks. But somewhere in the hospital's clinical odors, I caught a hint of something familiar. Something that made my chest tighten with an emotion I'd forgotten how to name.

The doctor treating my shoulder—a graying colonel with gentle hands—finished his examination and sat back.

"The shrapnel missed everything important. Clean wound, minimal tissue damage. You'll be fine physically in a week or two."

He paused, studying my face with attention that made me uncomfortable.

"But Lieutenant, you look like hell. When did you last sleep properly? When did you last laugh? When did you last feel anything besides tactical calculations?"

I opened my mouth to give the standard response—that I was operational, that I could return to duty immediately, that soldiers don't have the luxury of feelings in combat zones.

Instead, words came out that surprised me: "I need help, sir. Not just for my shoulder. For whatever this war has done to my head."

The colonel nodded slowly. "That's the first honest thing you've said since you arrived. Most officers aren't brave enough to admit when they're broken."

He wrote something on my chart, then looked up. "I'm ordering two weeks mandatory leave. Go home, Lieutenant. Remember what you're fighting to protect.

Remember who you were before the war tried to turn you into a machine."

Two weeks leave. The thought should have brought relief. Instead, it brought anxiety. What would I do with time that wasn't structured around fire missions and enemy contact? How do you live a normal life when your dreams are filled with crosshairs and your hands automatically calculate firing solutions for every elevated position you see?

And somewhere in the back of my mind, another question lurked: Would I have the courage to see her again? The woman whose vanilla scent still haunted my memory, whose pink tiffin box had been the only color in my black-and-white world of war?

The woman who might be the enemy agent trying to destroy everything I'd sworn to protect.

As I signed the leave papers with a hand that still trembled from weeks of accumulated violence, I realized I needed two kinds of doctors. One for the shrapnel wound in my shoulder that would heal in days.

And another for the deeper wounds in my heart that might never heal at all.

**Forty-seven days of steel and flame,*
Each dawn brought death like morning prayer.
Her pink box came through war's cruel game,
The only color in my nightmare.

Grid coordinates became my tongue,
Fire missions sang my heart to sleep.
Till shrapnel bit and I was flung
*From heights where souls grow dark and deep.**

CHAPTER 17

"BEFORE THE STORM"

September 20, 2014 – Home Leave

The smell of mustard flowers hit me like a gentle slap the moment I stepped off the bus in my village. Sweet, pungent, alive—so different from the metallic taste of cordite that had lived in my mouth for forty-seven days. My mother stood at the gate, her cotton saree wrapped snugly against the morning chill, tears already streaming down her weathered cheeks.

"Murari beta," she whispered, her voice cracking like old wood.

She reached toward my bandaged shoulder, then pulled her hand back, afraid to hurt me. But I could see the real damage wasn't the shrapnel wound—it was in my eyes. The same eyes that used to light up at her terrible cooking jokes now looked like they'd seen too much, felt too little.

"I'm okay, Ma," I lied, the words tasting like chalk.

Papa stood behind her, his retired soldier's hands clenched into fists. Not angry—helpless. The kind of helplessness that comes when your son returns from war carrying invisible wounds you don't know how to heal. He recognized the look in my eyes because he'd worn it himself once, decades ago 1999, "the Kargil Conflict."

The mustard fields stretched behind our house like a yellow carpet thrown across the earth. Every morning, I'd walk out there before sunrise and sit cross-legged among the flowers until the sun burned away the last of my nightmares. The ground felt solid under me—real dirt, not concrete bunker floors that shook with mortar fire.

Birds chirped overhead. Actual birds, not the whistle of incoming shells.

But my brain hadn't gotten the message yet. Every distant tractor engine sounded like artillery. Every car backfire made me drop to the ground, hands reaching for weapons that weren't there. The village kids would point and whisper: "That's the soldier who came back different."

They weren't wrong.

My sister Rajni found me there on the third morning, staring at nothing, mustard petals stuck in my hair.

"Bhaiyya," she said softly, settling beside me. "You're scaring the flowers."

Despite everything, my mouth twitched. Almost a smile.

"They've seen worse," I said.

"Have they?" She plucked a yellow petal and twirled it between her fingers. "Or have you?"

I couldn't answer that. The words got stuck somewhere between my brain and my tongue, like they were passing through too much scar tissue to make it out.

Every evening, Rajni made it her mission to make me laugh during dinner. Her jokes were terrible—the kind that make you groan before you chuckle. But she kept at it with the persistence of artillery fire.

"Bhaiyya, why did the army cook get promoted?"

I pushed dal around my plate, not really tasting it. "Why?"

"Because he finally learned to make food that wouldn't kill the enemy—just poison our own troops!"

Papa nearly choked on his roti. Ma swatted Rajni with her aanchal, but she was smiling too. And something inside my chest—some frozen part that had been locked away for weeks—cracked just a little.

The healing happened in millimeters. Like watching grass grow or wounds close. Some days I could almost taste my food. Some days I managed to sleep for three hours straight without dreaming of crosshairs and target coordinates.

On the seventh day, my phone rang at sunset. The caller ID made my breath catch: Susmita.

We'd been friends since class six at Sainik School Goalpara. She was the girl who could solve everyone's problems faster than me solving maths, who always knew when something was wrong before I said a word. There'd been something between us—not romance exactly, but something deeper. Like our souls were tuned to the same frequency.

"I've been having dreams about you," she said without preamble. Her voice carried that familiar directness that used to intimidate other cadets.

"Dreams?"

"Bad ones. Fire and smoke and you screaming. I woke up crying three nights in a row." Her breath caught. "Murari, what happened up there?"

My throat felt raw. Nobody had asked me that question yet. Not directly. Everyone tiptoed around it like stepping through a minefield.

"I learned how to kill people efficiently," I said finally.

Silence stretched between us, filled with everything we couldn't say over an unsecured phone line.

"Come home properly," she whispered. "Whatever part of you is still fighting that war, bring it home."

The words hit deeper than shrapnel. Because she was right—part of me was still up there, still calculating firing solutions, still waiting for the next incoming round.

"I'm trying," I said.

"Try harder. The world needs Lieutenant Murari, not this ghost you've become."

After fourteen days of mustard fields and terrible jokes and dreams that slowly changed from nightmares to something approaching normal sleep, the call came.

"Report back to duty, Lieutenant Murari," Major Isaac's voice crackled through my phone. "We need you at Mandi sector. Road opening duties from Mandi to Poonch bridge."

My stomach clenched. Back to Poonch. Back to checkpoints and constant vigilance and the endless calculations of who might be friend or enemy.

But also—back to her.

The bus ride back to Poonch took eight hours through winding mountain roads. With each kilometer, the landscape shifted from wheat fields to pine forests where men killed each other over lines drawn on maps. But it also brought me closer to something that made the killing feel purposeful.

I was protecting something worth protecting.

Mandi sector felt familiar and foreign at the same time. Same checkpoints, same mountains, same tension hanging in the air like smoke. But the briefings told a different story now. Increased terrorist activity. Three failed attempts to blow up Budha Amarnath temple. Grenade attacks on army convoys. Intelligence reports of heavily armed groups moving through the area.

"Situation's deteriorated since you left," Major Isaac informed me, his weathered face more lined than I remembered. "We've got Special Forces teams hunting in the mountains. Infantry doing daily search operations. And you—" he pointed at me with his pen, "—back to road security. Mandi to Poonch bridge. Every day, every vehicle, maximum vigilance."

"Understood, sir."

"Lieutenant." His voice dropped. "Personal advice? Keep your head clear. This sector's gotten more dangerous, not less. Trust your training, not your emotions."

The warning felt specific. Pointed. Like he knew exactly which emotions he was talking about.

My first patrol took me past the hospital where Jasleen worked. I slowed the jeep, scanning the parking area with professional interest, but my eyes were really searching for a flash of white coat, a familiar profile in the windows.

Nothing.

The road security routine came back like muscle memory. Check vehicles, scan for suspicious packages, maintain radio contact with checkpoints fore and aft. But underneath the mechanical precision, something had changed. The two weeks in mustard fields had reminded me why I was doing this work.

Not just to stop infiltrators or prevent attacks, but to protect a place where doctors could save lives without fear, where families could live without terror.

Where women could fall in love with soldiers without it being a crime against national security.

Three days back on duty, and I'd established a new routine. Morning patrol, afternoon checkpoint duty, evening security sweep. And every night, when the official duties ended, I'd find myself by the river that ran behind our base camp.

The water moved over rocks with a sound like whispered prayers. Fish jumped in the moonlight, their silver bodies catching starlight before disappearing back into the dark current. It was peaceful in a way that felt almost forbidden after months of violence.

I'd sit on the rocky bank, throwing pebbles into the water, watching the ripples spread in perfect circles until they faded into nothing. Each throw was like a small meditation—release the stone, watch it fly, listen for the splash, observe the consequences spread and disappear.

It was during one of these evening sessions, with the moon full and the water singing over stones, that my phone buzzed.

Major Isaac. Calling at 2130 hours. Nothing good ever came from calls that late.

"Sir?" I answered.

"Lieutenant, where are you right now?" His voice carried an urgency that made my spine straighten automatically.

"River bank behind base camp, sir. Evening... meditation."

"Listen carefully. We have actionable intelligence. Dr. Jasleen Kaur is compromised."

The pebble I'd been about to throw slipped from suddenly numb fingers.

"Sir?"

"Our reliable source confirms that she provided food, medical supplies, and treated terrorists operating in the area last night. But more concerning—" his voice dropped to almost a whisper, "—she was observed carrying an AK-47 magazine in her purse at 1900 hours today and driving away rapidly."

My vision blurred. The peaceful river sounds turned into white noise, like radio static in a bunker under bombardment.

"Sir, are you certain—"

"I'm tracking her location right now. GPS shows she just entered your base perimeter." His voice sharpened. "She's moving toward your quarters, Lieutenant. Right now."

"Lieutenant, do you copy? She's dangerous. Consider her armed and hostile."

I stood up from the river bank, legs unsteady. The moonlight that had seemed so peaceful moments before now felt like enemy illumination, exposing me to unseen threats.

"Copy, sir."

"Move to your quarters immediately. Your weapon is there. But approach with extreme caution—we don't know her intentions."

As I started walking toward the barracks, my mind raced through tactical calculations. Distance to my room: 200 meters. Cover available: minimal. If she was already inside, she'd have access to my weapons locker. She'd have the advantage of position and surprise.

But more than that—she'd have the advantage of my trust.

Every step toward my quarters felt like walking into an ambush. The familiar paths of the base camp looked different in the moonlight, shadows containing potential threats, corners hiding possible firing positions.

Then I saw him—Sepoy Rajesh, my buddy, walking toward my room carrying a tray with a glass of water. His AK-47 slung casually across his back like always, the weapon within easy reach of anyone who knew how to use it.

My blood turned to ice water.

Jasleen was in my room. If she really was what they said she was, she now had access to not just my personal weapon but a fully loaded assault rifle. One man's casual kindness could become everyone's death sentence.

I stopped walking, pressing myself against the wall of the radio bunker. My phone buzzed with a text from Major Isaac: "Confirm visual contact. Do not engage alone."

Through my room's window, I could see the warm glow of my desk lamp. A shadow moved across the light—definitely human, definitely female.

She was there. In my room. With access to enough firepower to kill half the men in this camp.

The woman I loved—or thought I loved—might be about to commit the kind of attack that would haunt the headlines for months. And I was the only one close enough to stop her.

But stopping her would mean accepting something that would shatter whatever was left of my ability to trust, to love, to believe in anything beyond the mechanical calculations of threat assessment and target elimination.

Academy training said: approach cautiously, assess the threat, neutralize if necessary.

My heart said: walk away. Let someone else handle this. Don't be the one who has to choose between duty and love.

But my legs were already moving toward my room, toward the woman who might be an enemy agent, toward answers I wasn't sure I wanted to know.

The wooden steps creaked under my boots as I approached my door. Inside, I could hear her voice—soft, musical, speaking to someone. On the phone? Or to Sepoy Rajesh?

My hand reached for the door handle, then hesitated.

Once I opened this door, everything would change. Either I'd discover that everything I'd believed about Jasleen was a carefully constructed lie, or I'd learn that our intelligence was wrong and an innocent woman was about to be destroyed by suspicion and fear.

Either way, the man who opened this door wouldn't be the same person who walked away from it.

I took a deep breath, tasting the mountain air one last time as someone who still believed in the possibility of love in a world at war.

Then I turned the handle.

**In mustard fields where childhood played,*
My mother's tears washed war away.
Rajni's jokes, though badly made,
Brought laughter back to each new day.

But duty called from mountain heights
Where tests of love and honor wait.
Between the pull of home's sweet lights
*And Kashmir's dark and twisted fate.**

CHAPTER 18

"TRUTH BEHIND THE VEIL"

September 30, 2014–2145 hour

I borrowed Sepoy Rajesh's loaded AK-47, my hands trembling slightly as I gripped the cold metal. Academy reflexes kicked in—safety off, finger finding the trigger, breath controlled. The wooden steps creaked under my boots like breaking bones in the mountain silence.

The door handle turned with a soft click that sounded unnaturally loud.

Rifle raised, sight alignment perfect—the black front post centered on Jasleen's face. Her dark eyes widened in shock, reflecting the barrel pointed directly at her.

"Don't move," I said, my voice sounding foreign to my own ears—cold, detached, military.

Her hands flew to her mouth, a strangled gasp escaping through her fingers. Her medical bag slipped from her shoulder, hitting the floor with a dull thud that scattered bandages like fallen leaves. I watched the color drain from her face, leaving her skin pale as moonlight.

"Murari," she whispered, my name barely audible.

Her body began to shake—not just trembling, but deep convulsions that started in her core and spread outward. Her knees buckled like someone had cut the strings holding her upright, eyes rolling back as consciousness started to slip away.

Without thinking, I lunged forward, catching her with my left arm while keeping the rifle ready with my right. She felt impossibly light, all strength gone from her muscles. Her head lolled against my shoulder, and I caught the faint scent of vanilla mixed with fear-sweat.

Through the window, I could see my two men, both with weapons raised like twin shadows of death. I held up my left hand, palm forward. Hold position. They nodded grimly but stayed ready to turn my room into a killing zone.

I half-carried, half-dragged her to my cot, my pulse hammering against my ribs despite my tactical training. Her pulse fluttered against my wrist—too fast, too weak, like a bird with a broken wing.

Her breathing came in sharp, shallow gasps. I dampened a towel with cold water and pressed it to her forehead. She flinched at the touch, eyelids fluttering like she was fighting her way back to consciousness.

"Easy," I said quietly. "Just breathe."

Her eyes fluttered open slowly, confusion clouding her features as she tried to remember where she was. Then her gaze found my face, traveled down to the rifle lying beside her, and fresh terror bloomed in her dark eyes like blood spreading through water.

Through the window, she could see my soldiers maintaining their deadly positions, rifle barrels glinting like hungry predators in the lamplight. Her breathing accelerated again—quick, desperate pants of someone drowning in fear.

I moved to the window and made a sharp downward gesture. Stand down, but stay ready. My men melted back into the shadows like professional ghosts, but I knew they remained poised to strike.

"Sit up slowly," I told her, my voice gentler now but still carrying military authority. "Don't make any sudden movements."

She struggled to rise, her body still betraying her with tremors that seemed to come from her very soul. I supported her back with one hand while reaching for water with the other. The glass rattled slightly as I held it to her lips—my own hands not as steady as I'd hoped. She managed a few small sips.

My phone buzzed. Major Isaac.

"Status?" One word.

I looked at Jasleen—really looked at her. The woman who had treated my soldiers without question, who had sent me food during the darkest weeks of my deployment.

"Green," I said.

The line went dead.

Jasleen's shoulders sagged with relief, but the fear remained in her eyes.

"You need to tell me what happened," I said, sitting across from her. "The complete truth."

She took a shaky breath, hands clasped tight in her lap.

"Last night, three men came to my house. All armed." Her voice was barely a whisper, like speaking louder might summon them back. "They demanded medical supplies—bandages, antibiotics, painkillers. Said they had wounded comrades."

I knew the look she was describing. The dead eyes of men who had crossed lines that normal people never approach, where violence becomes as natural as breathing.

"What did you do?"

"What could I do? When I hesitated, one showed me his AK-47." Her laugh held no humor, only the bitter sound of impossible choices. "I gave them what they wanted. They said I was part of their network now, whether I wanted to be or not. That people were watching me."

Tears began forming in her eyes, catching the lamplight like fractured diamonds.

"This evening, a small boy brought me a note. Maybe eight years old. He handed it to me and ran away before I could ask questions." She swallowed hard, her throat working against the words. "To collect what they'd left behind and deliver it tonight at 9 PM behind the government hospital."

"I found an AK-47 magazine on my kitchen table. Fully loaded."

"I panicked. I couldn't leave it at home—what if they came back? But I was too afraid to carry it." She looked up at me. "Then I saw your checkpoint. I thought if anyone would believe me, it would be you."

Without breaking eye contact, she reached into her purse and pulled out the magazine—thirty rounds of ammunition in curved steel. She placed it on my desk with a metallic click.

I examined it. Fresh oil, no wear marks, recently maintained.

I secured both the magazine and my rifle in my weapons locker. The simple act of putting away weapons changed the entire atmosphere from confrontation to conversation.

"What happens now?" she asked.

Exhaustion crashed over me like a dam bursting after too much pressure. Forty-seven days of combat, two weeks trying to piece together my shattered psyche, and now this—the woman I loved caught in a web that could destroy us both. I slumped forward, head falling into my hands.

"I don't know," I admitted, the words tasting like defeat.

She rose from the cot and moved toward me, her earlier terror replaced by something that made my chest tighten—concern, tenderness, the instinctive response of a healer seeing someone break apart.

"May I?" she asked softly, gesturing toward my hands.

I nodded, too exhausted for proper protocols.

Her fingers were warm against mine as she gently pulled my hands from my face. Her touch still carried that electric current that had nearly destroyed my military discipline months ago, but now it felt more like medicine than fire.

"You're exhausted," she said, studying my face with clinical precision that somehow felt intimate. "When did you last sleep properly? Your pupils are dilated. You're running on adrenaline and pure willpower, but both have limits."

"I can't sleep. Not with everything happening."

"What if you didn't have to sleep alone?"

The question hung between us.

"I'm terrified," she whispered. "Not just of those men, but of being alone tonight. Wondering if they're coming back, if I've failed some test I don't understand."

Her honesty cut through my defenses.

"If you could stay with me, just for tonight—it would help both of us."

I should have said no. Should have maintained protocols.

Instead, I nodded.

I dimmed the overhead light, leaving only my desk lamp. The softer glow made my room feel less like an interrogation cell.

Through the window, my men saw the light change and nodded understanding before disappearing into the darkness.

"There's something else," she said quietly, her voice carrying the weight of secrets too long held. "Something I should have told you months ago."

My stomach clenched like a fist closing around broken glass.

"I have family in Pakistan."

The words hit me like sniper fire—sudden, devastating, changing everything in an instant.

"My grandfather's brother settled in Muzaffarabad during Partition. His children and grandchildren still live there." She pulled out her phone with trembling fingers, showing me photographs that seemed to glow in the lamplight—faces that shared her smile, group photos of family gatherings separated by razor wire and political hatred.

"This is why intelligence reports show calls to Pakistan numbers. Why I'm seen meeting people at the border crossing. Why I carry packages back and forth."

Everything clicked into place with the mechanical precision of a rifle bolt sliding home. The suspicious communications. The border meetings. The money transfers that looked like terrorist funding.

"Family separated by Partition," I said, understanding flooding through me like cold water.

"We send medicine when someone is sick. Food during festivals. Money when jobs are lost." Her voice carried the weight of generations torn apart by lines drawn on maps by men who never lived with the consequences. "It's not politics, Murari. It's love that refuses to recognize borders drawn by strangers."

I stared at the photographs, seeing decades of divided families.

"Why didn't you tell me before?"

"Because I've seen what happens when people learn about cross-border family connections. Suddenly you're not a doctor—you're a security risk. Someone whose loyalty is questioned."

She was right.

"But tonight, when those men forced me into their network, I realized keeping secrets was destroying any chance of protecting people I love. On both sides."

I set down the phone, hands steadier now.

"There's something I need to tell you too. The army have been watching you for months. Every checkpoint, every patrol, every call and every money transfer, trying to understand who you really are."

"I know," she said softly. "I could feel it."

We sat in silence, months of unspoken truth settling between us.

"What happens tomorrow?" she asked.

"Tomorrow, you report the terrorist contact. We work together to set up protection. And we figure out how to navigate this without compromising anyone's safety."

She moved closer on the cot.

"And tonight?"

Academy training said maintain distance. Sleep on the floor. Keep weapons ready.

"Tonight, we help each other sleep."

She moved closer on the narrow cot, close enough that I could feel the warmth radiating from her body. Her hand found mine in the growing darkness, fingers intertwining with the certainty of surgical sutures.

"Murari?" she whispered.

"Yes?"

In the soft golden glow of my desk lamp, we found each other—not as soldier and suspect, not as interrogator and subject, but as two people who had been dancing around an inevitable truth for months. Her touch was gentle as she traced the worry lines around my eyes, her fingers speaking the words we couldn't say aloud.

"Are you sure?" I whispered against her forehead.

Her answer came not in words but in the way she drew closer, eliminating the last space between doubt and trust, between duty and desire. Time seemed to slow as we crossed the line we'd been approaching since that first night at the ceremonial dinner.

The lamp cast everything in warm amber light—her face soft with vulnerability, my hands warming as they found the curve of her cheek. What followed was gentle, wordless, a conversation conducted in whispered names and shared breath, two souls finding sanctuary in each other despite the war raging outside.

The concrete walls of my military quarters faded away. The weapons, the suspicions, the impossible circumstances—all of it dissolved until there was only this moment, this connection that felt both inevitable and miraculous.

Later, as she lay curled against me, her breathing deep and peaceful, I understood something I'd never learned in any military manual: sometimes the greatest act of courage isn't facing the enemy—it's allowing yourself to be completely vulnerable with another person.

Sleep came surprisingly easily—the first peaceful rest I'd had since returning from Mendhar.

At 0430 hours, my internal clock pulled me gently awake. Pre-dawn patrol would begin in thirty minutes. I had to be there—road security from Mandi to Poonch bridge, the routine that had become my anchor to normalcy.

I turned carefully, not wanting to wake her. The golden light of early dawn was beginning to creep through my window, painting everything in soft hues that made the harsh military setting seem almost beautiful.

Jasleen lay sleeping beside me, one hand tucked under her cheek, the other resting where my heart had been beating against her palm hours before. The morning light caught the gentle curves of her face, illuminating her features with an ethereal glow that made her look like something painted by the gods themselves.

Her hair spread across my pillow like spilled silk, catching highlights of gold and copper in the sunrise. Her lips were slightly parted in sleep, peaceful in a way I'd never seen before—all the tension and fear of recent weeks smoothed away by rest and trust.

I traced the air above her shoulder with my finger, not quite touching, not wanting to disturb this perfect moment. The light played across her collarbone, her neck, the elegant line of her jaw. Even in sleep, she was breathtakingly beautiful, but it was more than physical beauty—it was the peace in her expression, the trust she'd shown in allowing herself to be completely vulnerable with me.

I dressed quietly in the growing light, gathering my gear with practiced silence. Before leaving, I stopped to look at her one more time. The golden sunrise was painting everything in warm honey tones—her face, her hand where it lay against the pillow, the gentle rise and fall of her breathing.

This was what I was fighting to protect, I realized. Not just borders or national security, but moments like this. The possibility of love existing even in the midst of war. The hope that two people could find each other despite everything trying to keep them apart.

I placed a soft note on my field desk: "Gone to patrol. Back by 0630. You are beautiful in the morning light. Stay safe. -M"

The morning air was sharp and clean. My patrol route took me past the government hospital—empty parking lot, lone security guard. Intelligence had reported increased special forces activity in the area for operations to neutralize terrorists, and I had been tasked with guiding them as I knew the area and local community well.

At 0630, I returned to find my room empty, cot made with military precision, but a lingering trace of vanilla in the air that made my chest tighten with memory. A note on my desk in her precise medical handwriting: "Thank you for everything. Gone to hospital early to attend an emergency. Will call tonight. Stay safe. -J"

I showered, shaved, and reported for briefing feeling more human than I had in weeks. The combination of honest sleep and honest conversation had worked better than any medicine the army doctors had prescribed.

"Lieutenant, we have a situation developing," he said without preamble. "Special Forces detected three armed infiltrators moving toward the hospital sector last night. They were tracked to the government hospital vicinity before losing contact."

"Unknown. Hospital staff reported for normal duties this morning, including Dr. Kaur. But we lost the infiltrators around 0200 hours."

Three hours after Jasleen had left my room. Three hours after she'd trusted me with her deepest secrets.

"Recommendations, sir?"

"Full protective sweep of the hospital. Coordinate with local police. And Lieutenant—his voice carried a warning that cut through my chest like shrapnel, "maintain professional distance from civilian medical staff. Last night's developments don't change security protocols."

"Understood, sir."

But as I loaded my weapons and prepared for what felt like the most important operation of my life, I received a call from Mandi police post in charge. "Terrorist hiding inside Mandi government hospital. All men and women evacuated the hospital and are safe now. Only Dr. Kaur is inside, taken as hostage by terrorist."

If those men had been using Jasleen as an unwilling accomplice, and now realized she'd sought protection from Indian forces, her life wasn't just in danger—it was already forfeit.

The woman I loved was trapped inside that hospital with the same men who had threatened her the night before, and I might be able tosave her.

Or die trying.

My rifle felt heavier in my hands as I ran toward the vehicle, each step carrying me closer to a confrontation that would either end in rescue or tragedy. Everything we had shared—the trust, the vulnerability, the love that had finally bloomed between us—now hung in the balance with her life.

As my jeep roared to life and I sped toward the hospital, one thought echoed in my mind like artillery fire: I would not lose her. Not now. Not when I had finally found something worth fighting for beyond duty and country.

The final battle of my heart was about to begin.

> *My rifle found her frightened face,
> Then dropped as truth replaced my fear.
> She showed me love's most sacred space,
> Where trust makes everything unclear.
>
> Her family photos told the tale
> Of hearts divided by the fence.
> In golden light behind love's veil,
> We found our last sweet innocence.*

❧ ❧ ❧

CHAPTER 19

"THE FINAL SACRIFICE"

October 1, 2014–0800 hours

The government hospital stood like a fortress under siege. Police vehicles surrounded the building, their red and blue lights painting the morning air in urgent colors. Special Forces soldiers crouched behind concrete barriers, weapons trained on windows where death might appear at any moment.

I moved through the chaos with a singular focus, my rifle ready, every sense sharpened to combat clarity. The riverside entrance—that was my way in. The rear door that faced the small stream behind the hospital, away from the main siege perimeter.

Major Isaac's voice crackled through my radio: "Lieutenant, intelligence confirms three terrorists inside.

Dr. Kaur is being held in the main ward. Approach with extreme caution."

"Roger," I whispered, already moving along the riverbank.

The morning mist clung to the water like the breath of spirits, muffling my footsteps as I approached the hospital's rear entrance. Through the tall windows of the main ward, I could see movement—shadows shifting behind curtains, the occasional glint of metal.

Then I saw her.

Jasleen stood near the window, her white coat wrinkled and stained, her hands zip-tied behind her back. Even from fifty meters away, I could see the exhaustion in her posture, the way she held herself with quiet dignity despite her captivity.

Our eyes met through the glass.

For a heartbeat, the world stopped. Everything I'd felt the night before—the tenderness, the trust, the love that had bloomed between us—passed between us in that single glance. Her lips moved silently, and though I couldn't hear the words, I knew she was saying my name.

I held up my hand, palm forward. Stay calm. I'm coming.

She nodded almost imperceptibly, and then her expression changed. Terror flooded her features, and she began shaking her head frantically, trying to warn me about something I couldn't see.

The door.

Even from my position, I could see the thin wires running along the frame. An improvised explosive device—the terrorists had booby-trapped the entrance, turning my rescue route into a death trap.

I keyed my radio. "Contol, rear entrance is rigged. IED confirmed. Requesting EOD support."

"Negative, Lieutenant. No time. Terrorists are threatening to execute the hostage in ten minutes. You're authorized to proceed with immediate action."

Ten minutes. Not enough time for bomb disposal. Not enough time for backup. Just enough time for one desperate gamble.

I studied the door from my concealment. The blast radius would be maybe fifteen meters. If I could approach from an angle, use the concrete wall for cover, I might survive the initial explosion and fight my way through the smoke.

Might.

I began my approach, moving in tactical bounds from cover to cover. Twenty meters.

Through the window, I saw Jasleen watching my advance. Her face had gone pale as mountain snow, but her medical training was evident in how she assessed the situation. She could see the bomb wires from her position inside. She knew what would happen when that door opened.

Fifteen meters from the entrance, I paused to steady my breathing. This was it—the moment that would determine whether we both lived or both died.

I signaled my team to hold position and began my final approach.

"NO!"

The scream came from inside the building, piercing through glass and concrete. I looked up to see Jasleen throwing herself forward, breaking free from her captors through sheer desperation.

She reached the door before I could stop her.

Her hand hit the handle from the inside.

The world exploded.

Fire and metal erupted outward like the wrath of gods, turning the peaceful morning into a vision of hell. The blast wave reached us, showering us with debris and broken glass. I felt sharp fragments cut across my face and hands, heard Havildar Mehta curse as shrapnel grazed his right face.

But we were alive. Battered, bleeding from minor cuts, but alive.

The silence that followed the explosion was more terrifying than the blast itself.

"JASLEEN!"

My voice tore from my throat like broken glass. Through the smoke and ringing in my ears, I could hear the distant pop of gunfire as my team engaged the surviving terrorists inside the building.

I stumbled toward the destroyed entrance, my rifle ready but my heart already knowing what I would find.

The rear of the hospital was unrecognizable. The doorway had been obliterated, walls reduced to rubble, windows blown out in spider webs of shattered glass. And scattered across the debris field...

I stopped breathing.

What remained of Dr. Jasleen Kaur was spread across thirty meters of destroyed hospital ground.

"Sir." my buddy appeared at my elbow, his young face pale with shock. "The terrorists are neutralized. Building is secure."

I nodded mechanically, unable to tear my eyes away from the scene before us.

"Sir," he continued softly, "we need to... we need to collect..."

He couldn't finish the sentence. Neither could I.

Major Isaac's voice crackled through the radio: "Lieutenant, report status."

"Terrorist threat eliminated," I managed to say. "One civilian casualty."

Casualty. Such a small word for something so devastating.

"Sir," Havildar Mehta approached with a field stretcher and several body bags. His weathered face, which had seen decades of combat, looked stricken. "We'll handle this, sir. You don't need to—"

"No." The word came out sharper than I intended. "She saved my life. I'll do this."

What followed was the most horrific hour of my military career.

We moved through the debris field with the methodical precision that training had drilled into us, but every step felt like walking through my own soul being torn apart. Her white medical coat, now stained red and torn, hung from a piece of twisted metal. Her stethoscope lay bent and broken twenty feet away.

I found one of her hands—those gentle fingers that had traced worry lines from my face just hours before—still wearing the simple ring she'd worn since medical school. My vision blurred as I carefully, reverently, placed it in the body bag.

Piece by piece, we gathered what remained of the woman who had been my salvation, my torment, my love. Each fragment felt like a piece of my own heart being torn away. The golden hair that had caught sunlight in my room that morning. The hands that had healed countless patients without asking their religion or politics.

By the time we finished, I was shaking uncontrollably. Not from physical shock, but from a grief so profound it felt like drowning while still being able to breathe.

"Intelligence final report," Major Isaac's voice came through the radio as we completed the recovery. "Dr. Jasleen Kaur now have green status, had no connection to terrorist activities. Her cross-border communications were family related. She was completely innocent."

She had died not as a suspect or collaborator, but as a hero. A woman who had thrown herself onto a bomb to save the life of a soldier who had once pointed a gun at her face.

Within the hour, a military vehicle arrived carrying a wooden coffin draped in crisp white cloth. The sight of it—dignified, proper, befitting a hero—brought fresh tears to my eyes. At least she would go home with honor, not just as a casualty of war but as someone who had given everything for others.

We carefully transferred her remains into the coffin, and I placed her stethoscope—bent but not broken—on top, along with a small photo I found in her purse of her family on both sides of the border.

As if summoned by some ancient military ritual, soldiers began forming precise ranks around us. The chaos of battle had given way to the solemn ceremony of honoring the fallen.

Then I saw them approaching—four soldiers in perfect formation, their boots striking the ground in synchronized rhythm. Between them, they carried the Indian flag, the tricolor folded with mathematical precision according to military protocol.

The sound of their marching echoed off the hospital walls like a drumbeat for the dead. Each step bringing them closer to the woman who had earned this honor with her blood.

The four soldiers stopped beside the coffin, the flag held taut between them. In the morning sunlight, the saffron, white, and green seemed to glow with an inner fire.

They draped the flag over her still form with ceremony befitting a fallen warrior. The tricolor that represented everything she had lived for, everything she had died protecting, now covered the woman who had embodied the best of what our nation could be.

Colonel Ravi stepped forward, his weathered face solemn. "Dr. Jasleen Kaur served her nation as faithfully as any soldier. She died protecting others, as is the highest calling of both doctor and patriot."

Rifles rose in perfect unison throughout the assembled ranks. The bugle began to play—the haunting melody of "The Last Post," a song that had accompanied countless brave souls to their eternal rest.

"Fire!"

Twenty-one rifles discharged into the sky, their reports rolling across the valley like thunder. Each shot was a salute to Dr. Jasleen Kaur—healer, daughter, hero.

As the echoes faded, silence settled over the scene like a benediction. I approached the flag-draped coffin and knelt beside it, my hand resting on the tricolor that now covered the woman who had chosen my life over her own.

My tears fell onto the flag, each drop absorbed by the fabric that represented everything she had lived for, everything she had died protecting.

"I'm sorry," I whispered. "I'm so sorry I couldn't save you."

The woman I loved lay dead in my arms, her life extinguished in a moment of heroism that would never make the headlines, never earn the recognition it deserved. She had seen the trap, seen me walking into death, and chose to spring it herself rather than watch me die.

Jasleen had fulfilled every oath she'd ever taken. As a doctor, she had healed without question—even treating the wounds of terrorists who threatened her life. As a daughter of the soil, she had protected her homeland with her final breath. And as a woman in love, she had chosen my life over her own.

My heart had fallen on this battlefield, shattered beyond any possibility of repair. But in its breaking, it had learned the true meaning of courage, sacrifice, and love that transcends the boundaries of life and death.

The flag fluttered one last time in the mountain breeze, and I could swear I caught the faint scent of vanilla—her essence saying goodbye on the wind that would carry her memory across the valleys she had served so faithfully.

In Poonch valley where she healed until she died,
The coffin bore her while the mountains cried,
Though wars rage on and many more have tried,
Her love stands strong where fear and hate collide.

She saw the enemy with human heart,
And taught that healing was the greater art,
That understanding gives us all fresh start,
When souls connect despite what tears apart.

True heroism lives in what she knew,
That sacrifice makes broken spirits new,
She chose to save a life and see it through,
Her courage shows what love can really do.

The tricolor blessed her sacred name,
As sunset lit the valley's lasting flame,
Through sacrifice she conquered war and shame,
Her glory burns eternal, free from blame.